“I’m sorry we left . . . no idea you couldn’t take care of yourself.

Her head jerked up and her eyes flashed. “I can so take care of myself. I just didn’t know it was going to snow like this. I’d have gotten my supplies indoors sooner if I’d known.”

“What about the fire?”

Gathering a breath, she raised her arms and let them fall against her sides. “Well, yes, the fire is a problem. I suppose I should have watched how you made that one.”

Taken off guard by her sudden humility, Seth reached out and gripped her shoulder. The dog growled.

A smile tipped Ansley’s lips. “Maybe with him around, I won’t need a gun after all.”

The dog slunk to Seth’s feet, eyeing him like a bobcat would a weasel. Seth dropped his hand from Ansley’s shoulder and frowned. “You don’t have a gun?”

“Why, no. I’ve really never cared for them.”

“Well, out here, people carry guns. Especially women living alone. What if someone came to your door with ill intentions? How would you protect yourself?”

Her shoulders rose and fell in an infuriating shrug that proved she had no idea of the dangers of living out here. He wished he’d fought harder to keep her from moving into the cabin.

“I suppose the dog will protect me. After all, he got your hand off my shoulder just now, didn’t he?”

Books by Frances Devine

Love Inspired Heartsong Presents

A Touch of Autumn
Christmas on the Prairie

FRANCES DEVINE

grew up in the great state of Texas, where she wrote her first story at the age of nine. She moved to southwest Missouri more than thirty years ago and fell in love with the hills, the fall colors and Silver Dollar City. From an early age, the desire to be an author was instilled in her heart and she considers herself blessed to do what she loves. Frances is the mother of seven adult children and has fourteen wonderful grandchildren.

She is always happy to hear from her fans. Leave a comment at facebook.com/francesdevineauthor or email her at fldevine1440@gmail.com.

FRANCES DEVINE

Christmas on the Prairie

ISBN-13: 978-0-373-48736-3

Christmas on the Prairie

This edition published by arrangement with Love Inspired Books.

www.Harlequin.com

Printed in U.S.A.

Lo, children are an heritage of the Lord.
—*Psalms* 127:3

To my daughter, Tracey Bateman, who also happens to be my favorite author. Tracey, we both know this book couldn't have been written without you. Thanks for being such a wonderful daughter.

Chapter 1

Southern Kansas, 1871

"Rain's a-coming." The cowhand sitting next to Ansley Potter gave her arm a nudge and jerked his thumb toward the window. "Look over yonder."

Ansley shifted on the hard stagecoach bench, glancing around her seatmate to see the approaching storm. Black clouds to the west darkened the sky, and the wind had picked up quite a bit in the past few minutes, blowing cool air through the open windows. The breeze brought with it an odd combination of odors—cow manure and rain. Rain, Ansley enjoyed, the other, well, that she could live without. But both were preferable to the odor wafting from the man to her left.

For the past few hours, the incessant dipping and swaying of the stagecoach along fifteen miles of ruts in the well-worn path between Martin's Creek and Prairie Chicken, Kansas, had all but used up Ansley's good nature. The looming threat of bad weather wasn't helping much.

Being squeezed between Mr. Carson, the smelly cowhand, and a large mother of three impatient children was a barbaric way to get from one place to the next as far as Ansley was concerned. But she'd had little choice after disembarking the train that had brought her from Boston to Kansas.

Her sister's embrace at the end of the arduous journey would wash away every ounce of pain and aggravation. Of that, Ansley had no doubt. Playing the image of their reconciliation over and over in her head had been her only consolation for the past five hours.

Across the cramped space, a handsome man wearing a smart black suit kept his attention focused on a book, largely ignoring the rest of the riders. He was the only passenger who had not offered his name. Since boarding the stagecoach, Ansley had been trying to place him. Though he was engrossed in his book, she studied him, trying to remember where she'd seen his face before. As though sensing her perusal, he looked up and met her gaze. His lips curved into a cocky smile. Cheeks burning, she glanced away, wishing like anything she could escape the cramped space.

Next to him sat an elderly woman who had introduced herself as Mrs. Boatwright. The white-haired woman sat straight-backed, her hands folded demurely in her lap.

When the driver finally called out, "Prairie Chicken, two miles ahead," Ansley nearly wilted with relief. The young mother sighed, and Ansley could well imagine her trip had been more difficult with three children than Ansley's could possibly have been. The reading gentleman shut his book and laid the treasure in his lap, rubbing the cover as though he hated to leave the world within the pages. He glanced out the window, and Ansley noticed a one-inch scar slicing across his eyebrow.

The stagecoach rolled into town on the tail of another enormous clap of thunder that seemed to shake the ground beneath them. The skies opened and the misting rain became a torrent.

"Prairie Chicken," the driver yelled. In minutes, the swaying and rolling stagecoach stopped in front of what appeared to be a residence. The house loomed at least as large as Aunt Maude's, although it was clear time and neglect had weathered the structure.

"Here we are at last." Mrs. Boatwright secured her reticule to her wrist. "I left word with my housekeeper, Viola, to have a pot of stew and bread ready for anyone who might like lunch. The prices are fair and the food's as good as any."

The door opened, revealing the leathery driver. "Don't be all day about it, folks. I'm on a schedule."

The handsome man exited first, showing an utter lack of breeding that his demeanor and attire had thus far belied. Ansley couldn't help but be disappointed in him. What could a man like that possibly be doing in a town like Prairie Chicken, anyway? He certainly wasn't a cowhand. She'd say he was in his late thirties, if she had to guess. And apparently he possessed worse manners than the odious Mr. Carson.

The young mother hung back. "Please go ahead, Mrs. Boatwright."

The elderly woman shook her head. "You go on, Alice. The children have been cooped up long enough. Just walk right on in."

"Thank you." Alice reached out and squeezed Mrs.

Boatwright's hand, then turned to her children. "Be careful stepping down, Fiona. I'll hand Willie to you."

Ansley waited until everyone but Mr. Carson had exited. "After you, Miss Potter."

She slid toward the door, but he detained her with a dirty hand on her arm. "Wait."

Ansley noted his face had gone red. He worked his hat between his hands like a lump of dough. On the edge of the seat, his long legs folded until they were practically in his chest, and his precarious position amused Ansley. Clearly taking her smile as a sign of encouragement, the cowhand flashed a wide and toothy grin.

Ansley wished he hadn't.

"I was just wonderin' if I could come to call once yer settled and all."

Ansley pressed her fingers to the brooch at her throat. What on earth had she said during the past five hours to give this man any indication she would be amenable to such a request? "I'm grateful for the honor, Mr. Carson, but I am not in a position at the moment to receive callers."

"Oh, I know now ain't a good time. Why, I bet you don't even have a place to stay yet."

Thankfully, she was spared from answering by the driver, who cleared his throat loudly. "Let's go, folks." He held out his hand to assist her. Grateful for the reprieve, Ansley settled her hand in his and stepped down.

The door to Mrs. Boatwright's home was open, and the driver set Ansley's bag inside. She'd been forced to leave her trunks at the stage station in Martin's Creek until she could find a man to fetch them for her.

Ansley stepped inside the boardinghouse, hoping Mr. Carson wouldn't follow.

The hope was short-lived as he not only followed close on her heels but spoke over her shoulder.

"You was sayin' you'll allow me to call once you get settled?"

A gasp escaped Ansley. She'd said no such thing. "Mr. Carson…"

"I'd be honored if you'd call me Luke."

"Mr. Carson," she repeated with an edge of firmness. "I am here to visit my sister. I'm afraid I'll have very little time to accept gentleman callers."

"Yer sister, you say? Who might that be?"

Honestly, could the man not take a hint? "It just so happens her name is Rose Potter—er—Dobson."

A frown creased his brow. "Potter-Dobson. I don't know her." Just as Ansley was about to correct the misunderstanding about Rose's name, his face brightened and he snapped his fingers. "You mean Rose Dobson? Married to Frank?"

If he knew Rose and Frank, this annoying man might possibly be of some help. "Precisely."

"Well, what do you mean yer here to visit Rose? Ya mean Seth?"

"Seth? I'm afraid I don't know anyone by that name." Ansley pressed her fingers to her temple to quell a sudden ache. "Mr. Carson, may I impose upon you to take a message to my sister?"

"I wish I could do that, miss. It just ain't possible."

Ansley gaped at the man. All day long he'd done nothing but attempt to get in her good graces, and now when she asked a favor he actually refused? "It's of no consequence. I'll find another way."

Mr. Carson continued as though she hadn't spoken. "Miss Potter," he said again, "I sure hate bein' the one to tell you this, but Miss Rose is gone."

"What do you mean, gone?"

Of course, she hadn't corresponded with her sister in years. Aunt Maude had been so angry over the marriage, she'd confiscated and destroyed all of Rose's letters for the past decade. Only her deathbed and fear of missing the pearly gates had made Aunt Maude confess. If Rose had moved away, how would Ansley ever find her again?

Luke averted his gaze to the floor, and a knot of dread began to form in Ansley's gut.

"Please, Mr. Carson. What is it?"

Slowly, he lifted his gaze to hers, sorrow clouding his eyes. "Miss Potter, yer sister and her husband was killed nigh on to four months ago. I can't say how sorry I am to have to tell you that."

Ansley stared at him as the room moved around her. She hadn't heard right, that was all. Though the tears forming in her eyes were proof she had.

Her Rose. After ten years, Rose had died believing Ansley hadn't cared enough to answer even one of her letters.

Seth Dobson flipped up the collar on his coat and adjusted his hat against the pouring rain as the horses labored in the mud. In a town the size of Prairie Chicken, word spread pretty fast, so he already knew from Luke Carson that Frank's sister-in-law had arrived. And he knew she'd come to town expecting to be reunited with Rose. The reminder of his brother and sister-in-law and their untimely deaths brought back a rush of grief that had just begun to abate in the first place. He could imagine how Rose's sister must be feeling. His heart went out to the woman he'd yet to meet.

He pulled on the reins and the wagon rolled to a stop in front of Mrs. Boatwright's boardinghouse.

Seth's stomach seized as he wiped his feet on the mat outside the front door. The Boatwright boardinghouse and restaurant always smelled of fresh baking and whatever Viola King, Mrs. Boatwright's cook, was preparing for the evening meal. There was no need to knock, as the boardinghouse and restaurant used the same door. A bell above the door dinged to announce his arrival.

Mrs. Boatwright appeared within a minute. "So you've heard."

"Yes, ma'am." Seth swallowed hard, fidgeting with his wet hat.

"Shall I fetch Miss Potter for you? She's been quite distraught since that fool Luke Carson blurted out the news of Rose and Frank's death.

"Yes, ma'am."

"Well, get settled in the parlor while I inform Miss Potter you're here. Don't sit on anything cloth with your wet clothes."

Seth heaved a sigh and walked the distance from the foyer to the parlor. He started to sit in a wooden rocking chair next to the fireplace, but he noted the fire was little more than glowing coals. The rain had arrived with a cooling wind, and the air in the old house felt damp and cold, which probably wasn't good for Mrs. Boatwright's aching bones. He grabbed a poker next to the hearth and jabbed at the coals, then added wood from the box next to the fireplace. In minutes, the fire blazed. He walked toward the rocker but stopped at the sound of a woman's voice.

"Hello?"

He straightened at the sight of a young woman standing in the doorway. She appeared refined and citified, just as Luke Carson had described her. Her hair was brown. He couldn't tell the color of her eyes from this distance, but the shape of her face, though not as plump, resembled Rose's. Rose had also been quite a bit shorter than her sister. And if he had to guess, though he'd never say it aloud, this one was a few years older. Where Rose had been pleasant looking and fun, this sister was pretty to the point of beautiful. Something jumped in his stomach, and for a moment, Seth could do nothing but stare.

"Mr. Dobson?" Her tone was husky and low, soft and barely above a whisper, but enough to jerk him from his stupor.

Seth cleared his throat and gestured toward the rose-colored wing chair across from his. "Please come in. Miss Potter, I take it?"

"Yes, and you are—were—my sister's brother-in-law?" She walked—no, glided was more like it—across the room as she spoke and sat in the seat he offered. "It's a pleasure to meet you, Mr. Dobson." Her eyes and nose were red. Obviously she had been crying.

"Likewise. I'm sorry you came all this way to discover the sad news." Seth sat in the wooden rocker and searched for words.

"Thank you, Mr. Dobson. Your loss is no less than mine."

"Your husband didn't travel with you?" The question seemed kinder than directly asking about her spinsterhood. And he had to know if she was already taken.

At the sight of the sudden frown creasing her brow, Seth inwardly kicked himself for being so stupid. His ears heated up.

But she seemed to recover and shook her head. "The fact is I am not married. After Rose left, there was only me to take care of Aunt Maude."

"Is that what caused the trouble between you two?"

The frown returned. "I assure you there has never been, nor could there be, a smidge of trouble between my sister and myself." Her voice broke.

Fishing a clean, folded handkerchief from his coat pocket, he leaned forward and offered it to her. She eyed the cloth and then accepted it. "Thank you, Mr. Dobson."

"Miss Potter, I didn't mean any offense." He weighed the idea of assuring her that her age had done nothing to diminish her beauty and that all the men in Boston must be fools. But he knew, though he wasn't sure how, that she wouldn't appreciate the effort.

"What makes you think there was trouble between us? I certainly can't imagine Rose believing such a thing, much less confiding the idea to anyone."

Seth smiled. "You're right. She never said a thing. I have been raising Frank and Rose's children since they...died." He swallowed around the hateful word. "I found dozens of letters Rose wrote to you—returned. The children told me she cried every time one came back."

"I assure you," she said with a gulp. "If I'd known about them, I'd have answered every single one." She dabbed at the tears on her cheeks. "Our aunt returned them. I didn't know where Rose lived until this summer. It must have been just prior to her death. Poor Rose died thinking the worst of me." Her tears spilled over. Helpless panic rose inside of Seth.

"But why did you wait so long to come?"

Miss Potter squared her shoulders. "As I said, my aunt returned all the letters. I didn't have an address. All I knew was the information Rose gave me the night she snuck off to marry Frank. That they were to be married and she was moving to Kansas. She didn't even tell me the name of this town, though I can see why."

"How did you find out she lived in Prairie Chicken?"

"I hired an investigator. And since all the information I could give him was their names and that she lived in Kansas, it took some time for him to locate them." She sent him a quivery smile. "When I finally received news of their whereabouts in early July, I sent a letter straightaway, but I guess I was too late." If only she'd come as soon as she'd discovered where Rose was, instead of waiting to get Aunt Maude's affairs in order.

"Did it occur to you Rose might have been angry and chosen not to answer?"

Again, her lips turned up at the corners. She shook her head. "Never once did that possibility cross my mind. Rose was never the sort to hold a grudge. On a whim, I sent a telegram the morning of my departure from Boston. I suppose now I know why there was no one to greet me when I disembarked the stage."

Seth sucked in a breath, waiting for her tears to resume. Instead, she tilted her head and peered at him. "Mr. Dobson, did you say my sister had children?"

Chapter 2

After a fitful night's sleep, Ansley's head still swam with the notion that darling Rose had borne three children without her family—namely, Ansley herself—to help her. Mr. Dobson had promised to bring them over after school today. But she had some things to do before meeting her nephew and two nieces.

Shaking off the fuzzy early-morning web clouding her brain, she stretched her arms above her head. A smile tipped her lips as she heard Alice trying to quiet the Anderson children outside her bedroom door. "Hush before you wake Miss Potter. Come, let's go downstairs and offer our assistance to Mrs. Boatwright and Mrs. King."

"Chores?" A trio of groans grew faint as the little family moved toward the stairs.

"Yes. Mrs. Boatwright has been very kind to us. The least we can do is help out."

Ansley shoved the thick quilt aside, fully intending to rise, dress and go down to join the breakfast preparations. Instead, she closed her eyes, just for a second. The lack of sleep caught up to her, and she felt herself drifting, unable to pull herself from the fog. The last thing she saw before sleep claimed her again was Mr. Dobson's handsome face as he told her all about Rose's darling children.

A loud knock at her door jerked her awake and she sat up, instantly alert.

"Miss Potter?" Mrs. Boatwright's stern voice pierced the closed door.

Pulling the covers to her shoulders, Ansley called for the proprietress to enter.

Mrs. Boatwright opened the door and walked inside carrying a tray. "Do you intend to sleep the day away?"

"No, of course not." Ansley's face warmed under the condemnation. "I must have fallen back asleep."

"Well, no matter. As you can see, I've brought your breakfast." She set the silver tray on the writing desk along the far wall. "But don't expect this each morning. Breakfast is served in the dining room promptly at seven. Next time, you'll have to do without until lunch."

"Of course. How thoughtful of you."

"I'll leave you to your breakfast. Alice's children have requested books from my library and I promised to show them all the stories I read to my sister's children when they were young. We'll expect to see you at noon in the dining room."

"Wait, Mrs. Boatwright."

"Yes?"

"I need to send a telegram today." She found it difficult to meet the woman's eyes, fearing Mrs. Boatwright might just see right through to her soul.

"And?"

"Well, it's just that I don't know where to find the telegraph office."

Mrs. Boatwright chuckled. "Prairie Chicken is no Boston, Miss Potter. Just turn left at the bottom of the porch steps and keep going. It's just next to the general store. You'd best hurry, though. Looks like we're in for another gully washer."

"I will, and thank you."

"You're welcome." She reached for the doorknob but turned back. "Miss Potter, you might get to know Seth and Teddy before you go trying to yank those young'uns away from them."

"Why, Mrs. Boatwright, I'd never do that."

And who on earth was Teddy? Another brother?

The old lady's eyebrows lifted and Ansley could see she didn't believe it.

With a sigh of concession, Ansley waved her hand. "I'm simply going to apprise my lawyer of the situation and inquire as to my rights concerning Rose's children."

"Frank and Rose left them to Seth. He's been good to them."

Ansley's defenses rose. After all, they'd had no idea she would want them. "I'm sure he has, but I have to believe my sister would have wanted me to raise her children."

"Why would you think that? You haven't spoken to her in ten years."

How dare she? The old lady must've been eavesdropping the night before. The very thought raised Ansley's ire quite a lot. She gathered a breath for control before she spoke. "Through no fault of mine or Rose's, I assure you. Rose had the benefit of an education and culture. Her children should have the same. If she were here, she would attend to those things. But with her gone, things have changed." She paced the floor. "I mean, honestly, Mrs. Boatwright. Tell me, who in this town is going to teach the children about music, literature, art?"

Mrs. Boatwright narrowed her gaze. "There are other things they will learn here. Things I highly doubt they could learn in a fancy city school. Such as hard work, love and the support of good friends in a small community. And it isn't as though there's no schoolteacher. They certainly aren't growing up ignorant."

Though the woman did make a couple of good points, Ansley refused to back down. "There are different levels of ignorance. If they're to make good matches, they must learn certain graces."

Mrs. Boatwright snorted just like that. "Matches? They're children. Do you intend to force them into arranged marriages?"

"Of course not!" But for Rose's girls to marry farmers and consign themselves to the hard lives of farm wives when there was simply no reason for them to do so simply wouldn't do. Ansley quickly dismissed the thought that shoved its way into her mind: Rose had married a farmer, and it appeared as though she had been completely content with her life.

"Besides, dear, all your schooling didn't exactly make a good match for you, did it?"

Heat raced to Ansley's cheeks. "Well, no. But I had my aunt to care for and no time for courting and such."

Shaking her head, Mrs. Boatwright reached for the door again and turned the knob. "I suppose there's no changing your mind."

"No, ma'am, there isn't. And I'd appreciate it if you'd keep this between us."

"I can see why you would."

Uneasiness gripped Ansley's stomach. "I'd just prefer to discuss any arrangements with Mr. Dobson before he gets the wrong impression."

"Well, you needn't worry. My lips are sealed. Trust me, I wouldn't want to be the one to speak to Seth and Teddy about them losing those children. And the children probably wouldn't find the idea very pleasing either. They love their uncle and aunt." She paused as though she might go on, then opened the door. "Good day, Miss Potter."

Alone with the smell of bacon, eggs and coffee, Ansley stared at the closed door. Aunt Teddy? She'd assumed "Teddy" was a man. Mr. Dobson hadn't mentioned having a wife. But she supposed it was natural for a handsome man such as himself to have been snatched up long ago. Nibbling on a slice of crisp bacon, Ansley chided herself at the gnawing disappointment deep inside.

Gracious, she didn't even know the man. Besides, once she informed him of her intentions regarding the children, he would hate her forever.

Seth halted the wagon in front of the schoolyard just as the dismissal bell rang. A moment later, the doors flew open and children poured out of the building. Frowning, he peered closer through the pouring rain, hoping to catch a glimpse of at least one of the children.

"Uncle Seth!" Jonah had spotted him. The nine-year-old waved, and then nudged his little sisters toward the wagon. Seth hopped down and walked to the other side.

Five-year-old Lily greeted him with her usual heart-melting smile, and held up her chubby arms. Seth carried her around to his side of the wagon and set her in the seat before climbing in next to her. Jonah hopped into the back, his legs dangling from the tailgate. "Jonah," Seth called. "Come up here. I need to tell you three something."

Seth flicked the reins and headed the wagon toward the boardinghouse.

"You're going the wrong way, Uncle Seth."

"We're going to Mrs. Boatwright's," he said, glad for the introduction to the subject.

"For pie?" Lily's voice rose with childish excitement. The pudgy little girl had a sweet tooth like no child Seth had ever met.

He chuckled. "Maybe. If you're good. But there's another reason we're going there. There's someone I want you to meet."

"Who?" Lily asked.

Jonah gave a snort. "I bet Uncle Seth's getting hitched."

Seth jerked his head around to look at the boy. "What on earth gave you that idea?"

"Sarah Wayne said her aunt Isabelle is setting her cap to get you to the altar."

Well, that was news to him. He'd never even considered Miss Isabelle Wayne in that way. "Well, you already know Miss Isabelle, so even if I were sweet on her, which I'm not, why would I be taking you to meet her?"

Hannah glanced over Lily's head. "Then who are you getting married to, Uncle Seth?"

The horses gave a sudden jerk as one of them slipped, then righted itself in the sludge. Grateful for the quick reprieve from the ridiculous line of questioning, Seth muscled the animals back in line. "Okay, listen up. I'm not getting married. There is no woman for you to meet. Well, there is, but she's not someone I'm marrying."

"Are you courting her? First you have to court her, and then you get to marry her." Lily continued the completely inappropriate conversation that was, quite frankly, starting to wear on Seth's good nature. "That's what Sarah Wayne says." Clearly, the children believed Sarah Wayne to be an authority on the subject of courting and marriage. He might have to have a talk with the schoolteacher about this Sarah Wayne.

"No. I'm not courting anyone. I'm not marrying anyone. The woman you are going to meet is your ma's sister."

"Aunt Ansley?"

Jonah's question brought Seth's attention back around to the boy. "Yes. How much do you know about her?"

Hannah answered. "Mama told us all about how she had a sister and the two of them lived with a very rich aunt after their ma died when they were children. She said she missed her sister something awful, and sometimes Mama cried about it."

"Why is she here?" Jonah asked, his voice thick and accusing.

Seth pulled on the reins, halting the wagon in front of the boardinghouse. He set the brake and wrapped the reins around it, then turned his attention back to a question he wasn't sure how to answer. "I don't know. But she didn't know your Ma and Pa aren't here anymore." He couldn't bring himself to say the word "dead."

Lily nestled against his arm and looked up, her beautiful green eyes filled with uncertainty. "Will she like us?"

Seth pulled her onto his lap. "How could she not?"

"I don't care if she likes me," Jonah said. "I don't like her."

Hannah responded before Seth could reprimand the boy. "You don't even know her."

"So? She made Ma cry. Are you going to like someone who made Ma cry?"

"I don't know."

Seth drew in a breath and released it. "Well, let's wait to pass judgment until we give her a chance at least."

With the little girl in his arms, he maneuvered carefully, stepping out of the wagon into two inches of mud. "Be careful getting down," he instructed Jonah. "And help Hannah."

Mrs. Boatwright met them at the door and ushered them inside out of the rain.

"Well, the children are soaked to the skin, aren't they?" She looked them over in her stern way and jerked her head toward the dining area through a door to the right. Her gaze focused on Lily, who was still in Seth's arms. "I'd say you'd like to have a slice of my apple pie, wouldn't you?"

Lily glanced up at Seth. "Have I been good?" He smiled and set her on the floor. "I guess so."

Mrs. Boatwright inclined her gray head. "Tell Mrs. King I said you can each have a slice of whatever pie you'd like and a glass of milk." She pointed to a table where two children were already sitting. "Those two came in on the stage with me yesterday, and they'll be living in town. The girl is just about your age, Hannah. What if the three of you go and sit with them and introduce yourselves?"

The three headed toward the door. Mrs. Boatwright frowned. "Have you nothing to say to me, children?"

They stopped and turned guiltily. "Thank you for the kind offer of pie, ma'am," Hannah said, giving a small curtsy. "We'll go and make our introductions, as you suggested."

Mrs. Boatwright remained focused on Hannah as the trio headed to the dining room. "She's an odd little thing, isn't she?"

Her words raised Seth's defenses. "I don't think she's odd. Just easily influenced." Seth made a mental note to speak with Teddy, as soon as she returned from visiting their grandfather in Martin's Creek. Clearly she read the girl far too many fairy stories.

"Well, don't go getting riled up," the elderly woman said. "I didn't mean her mind's unhinged. Just that she's different from other little girls."

"Not the ones who curtsy." Seth couldn't stop a smile.

With a wave of her hand, Mrs. Boatwright dismissed the topic. "Shall I fetch Miss Potter for you? I assume you've brought the children to meet her?"

"Yes, ma'am. Thank you."

"Wait here," Mrs. Boatwright instructed.

Seth stood at the bottom of the steps watching the children through the adjoining door between the foyer and restaurant. He heard a door close at the top of the stairs. He turned just as Miss Potter began descending the steps. Just like the day before, she wore a dress far too fancy for Prairie Chicken, but he had to admit, it was nice to see a woman all fancied up and looking pretty—like one of those princesses in England. She smiled down at him as each step brought her closer. "Good afternoon, Mr. Dobson." When she reached the bottom of the steps she extended her hand.

He raised the hand and just as he pressed his lips to the soft fingers, he realized she had only meant to shake his hand.

He met her startled gaze. "Why, that was unnecessary, Mr. Dobson."

Sending her a sheepish grin, he shrugged and let go of her hand. "You looked awfully royal coming down the stairs. It just seemed like the thing to do."

"You're mocking me?" A little frown creased her brow and Seth recognized a look of hurt rather than anger.

"No, Miss Potter. You just looked pretty and walked so—I don't know."

"Gracefully?" Mrs. Boatwright supplied, her voice thick with amusement.

"Yes, that's the word. You looked graceful." Oh, for mercy's sake. He was just making himself look like more of a fool with every word he spoke. "Anyway, I'm sorry for making you uncomfortable. I don't think I've ever kissed a lady's hand in my whole life."

Of course, he'd never met a woman as refined and soft-spoken as Ansley, either. And here she was just staring at him as though he'd lost his mind.

Then, suddenly, she laughed. Loudly. Not the sort of laugh he imagined might come out of a princess. By the sound of it, he wouldn't have been a bit surprised if she'd slapped him on the back. "Mr. Dobson, I assure you I was only a little surprised. So tell me, where are my sister's children?"

Chapter 3

Ansley fought a rush of tears as she stood in the doorway to the dining room and watched the three children sitting at a table with the two eldest Anderson children. Three bedraggled darlings who looked just like Rose—especially the youngest girl. "They're soaked," Ansley murmured.

"I collected them from school in the wagon, but it was raining pretty hard."

At his defensive tone, Ansley hurried on to clarify. "It wasn't a criticism, Mr. Dobson. Just an observation. I'm sure a little rain isn't going to hurt them."

The boy, her nephew, shoved back his empty plate and gulped down the milk in his glass. He turned and his eyes found his uncle, then slid over to her. He stared, unsmilingly. Alarm seized Ansley at the anger flashing in his eyes.

"That's Jonah, the oldest," Mr. Dobson said, his voice low. "Don't worry, he'll come around."

Ansley simply nodded. For the life of her, she couldn't fathom why Rose's son should be angry with her.

The boy said something to the girls and both turned. As she would have expected of any child raised by Rose, the children immediately stood and made their way across the room.

"Children, this is your aunt Ansley."

Unable to look away from the children standing before her, she smiled and held out her hand to the boy, whose tongue was working a line of milk over his lip. "I'm your mama's big sister."

The boy sized her up, unblinking. "We know who you are."

"Jonah." Mr. Dobson's tone revealed his disapproval.

"Jonah has his reasons, Mr. Dobson. I'm sure we'll talk our way through them when he's ready."

The boy's eyebrows went up. He stepped back and pushed the smallest girl forward. "This is Lily, the baby."

"I'm not a baby!" Her fists clenched and Ansley felt an immediate kinship with the little girl. Ansley had been the fighter between Rose and her, the unapologetic defender of the weak and put-upon.

"Of course you're not a baby." Ansley bent forward and met the child eye-to-eye. "I think your brother just means you're the youngest. And there's nothing at all wrong with being the youngest. Look at your mama. She was my little sister just like you are to Jonah and…" She didn't know the middle child's name.

"Hannah," the girl supplied. She gave a perfect curtsy. "Pleased to meet you, Auntie Ansley. Mama said you had the most beautiful name she ever heard and she used to be jealous because her name was just plain Rose."

So she had spoken to the children about her childhood. How much did they know? "Can I tell you a secret, Hannah?"

The child nodded, her eyes wide.

"Your mama's name was not 'just plain Rose' and I was always jealous of her name, too."

"You were?"

Ansley nodded at her captive audience. "When Rose was born, my parents—your grandparents—were surprised to welcome another baby girl. They had been expecting a boy, so they hadn't prepared a name for your mother. But the day she was born, my papa clipped a bud from Mama's rosebush and from that day on, he always called your mama his little rosebud." She swallowed past a lump. "I always believed she had the most beautiful name in the world."

Lily slipped a warm, pudgy hand into Ansley's. "I like that story, Auntie Ansley."

Relief flooded over her. At least the girls were inclined to open their hearts to her. Perhaps Jonah would in time.

She faced Mr. Dobson, drawing a long breath. "May I speak with you in private?"

"Of course." He turned to the children. "Go back to your table for a few minutes. I'll collect you shortly."

The children did as they were told, but it was clear from the long-suffering expressions on their faces—at least the girls'—exactly how they felt about being dismissed.

Ansley's heart sang at the knowledge that not only had Rose borne children, but that they were wonderful, imaginative, mostly polite children. Perhaps the boy would come around. Or if not, was it possible Mr. Dobson might consider allowing her to return to Boston with just the girls? She believed she could win over the girls easily. The boy might resent her even more if she tried to take him away.

Seth's hand cupped her elbow. "Shall we return to the parlor?"

She nodded and he released her. Once they returned to the room, Seth went to the fire and poked the logs that had begun to burn away. The fire sparked as he added another log and turned to her. "I reckon we have some talking to do."

"Yes." Ansley picked at nonexistent lint on her skirt and swallowed hard. "Tell me about your family. Do the children see their grandparents often?"

Mr. Dobson shook his head. "My ma died a few years back. Pa joined her within a year. Now it's just me and my sister, Teddy, plus our grandpa, who lives in Martin's Creek. The children live with Teddy and me."

Sister! So he didn't have a mother for the children. Of course a sister was almost as bad. A lone man might welcome the relief of having the children taken off his hands, but a woman was another story. This Teddy might prove to be a problem. Still, Ansley had to try. She would love nothing more than to pack up the three of them and take them back to Aunt Maude's home in Boston. After all, the home belonged to her now, along with an inheritance large enough to keep them all well dressed and well fed, and to allow them to attend proper schools. Surely Mr. and Miss Dobson would see how much better off they'd be with her.

But as she returned Mr. Dobson's gaze, his narrowed eyes indicated he might have an inkling what she was up to.

She gathered a breath and clasped her fingers together so tightly her knuckles turned white. "Mr. Dobson. I came to this town with the intention of reuniting with my sister. I assumed there might be children, but I would never have imagined they would be orphaned."

"They have me."

"Yes, of course they do, and from the appearance of things, they're being cared for in the way Rose would have wanted. However…"

"You want them." He spoke the words without inflection.

"Yes. I am well able to provide for them. And they'd be loved like no other children were ever loved."

"The way you and Rose were after your folks passed on?" Gone was the man who had, only moments before, kissed her hand and told her she was pretty and graceful. Mr. Dobson's voice had grown combative. And though she preferred the former, Ansley knew how to hold her own, and she squared her shoulders.

"No. My aunt was a self-centered, bitter spinster, incapable of putting anyone's needs above her own. And while she loved us in her own way, she loved herself more."

"You're a spinster. How do I know you aren't just like the old woman?" He stood, paced the room. "And how do I know you wouldn't raise the children as strict and cold as you were raised?"

Hearing herself compared to Aunt Maude made Ansley's blood run cold. In the past few months, there had been a steady stream of suitors, all after her inheritance, all bitter over her rejection. And almost all had voiced similar words to Mr. Dobson's last. They claimed she'd be nothing more than a bitter old spinster, suspicious of anyone who might try to love her. She would die alone with her money and big house with no one to mourn her. Ansley refused to believe that. Even if she never married, she would not live a life of indifference.

"I know I will raise the children differently, Mr. Dobson, because I am different. My aunt had no love for her brother, my papa. He was rather a disappointment to the family. But I loved my sister and I love her children. Love makes the difference."

"I love them, too, Miss Potter. So does Teddy. And just so we're clear, those kids don't even know you. They love us. I won't give them up." He had stopped pacing and his jaw was tight and determined. "You're welcome to see them anytime you'd like, but I made Rose and Frank a promise, and I intend to see it through."

Ansley saw the certainty in his eyes and knew she was in for a fight. But she wasn't foolish enough to press the issue and risk raising his ire any more. If she could spend time with the children, there was always a chance Mr. Dobson would eventually have a change of heart. Tomorrow she would telegraph her housekeeper and let her know she would be spending the holidays right here in Prairie Chicken. Two months should be long enough to convince Mr. Dobson of the wisdom in her plan, and if not, it would be long enough for her lawyer to start the process of her gaining legal custody.

The rain had stopped by the time Seth gathered the children and herded them out to the wagon, amid the girls' loud protests over leaving their aunt Ansley. Only a promise from Seth and Miss Potter that she would come to dinner the following evening convinced them to obey. The excited chatter all the way home grated on his nerves, and relief flooded him as he pulled up to the two-story frame home his pa had built. Smoke wafted from the chimney. Teddy must have gotten home from Grandpa's after all.

"Get on with your chores," he instructed, leaving the

wagon for Jonah to put away. Hannah went to tend the milk cows, and Lily, the chickens. "And be sure to take off your shoes before you come inside or Aunt Teddy will have all our heads."

As relieved as he felt that Teddy had made it back safely, he had a lot of thinking to do after his conversation with Miss Potter. Once the children came in from their chores, all they'd be talking about was their new aunt, so he supposed he'd best fill Teddy in before that happened. His stomach hadn't stopped churning since Ansley Potter had announced the children would be better off with her in Boston.

"What am I going to do about her, Lord?" He waited for a sense of peace to come as it usually did when he prayed, but this time, his stomach continued to churn, and he received no answer from above.

Opening the door and stepping inside, he was greeted by the aroma of supper cooking on the stove. "That you, Seth?" Teddy called from the kitchen, and then appeared in the doorway, her hair damp and laying around her shoulders.

Seth removed his hat and dropped it onto the hook by the door. "You were supposed to be home yesterday. What happened?"

She shrugged. "I missed the stage so I thought I'd catch it today. But Grandpa had a little fall and twisted his ankle. By the time the doc said he'd be okay, it was too late. I borrowed one of Grandpa's horses. I was soaked clean through by the time I got ten miles. But I figured a little rain wouldn't hurt me, so here I am. Besides, it's faster on horseback."

"How is he?"

"Oh, his ankle will be fine in a couple of days. Rachel Conroy is going to check on him and take him food until he's back on his feet."

"That's good." Seth peered closer. Sometimes Teddy said more in what she didn't actually say in words, and he could tell there was something else.

"What else?"

She sent him a scowl. "How do you always do that?" A deep sigh shoved out of her throat. "He's worried about Frank's land." She angled a rueful glance at Seth. "Sorry. He dragged it out of me."

"Great, all we need is Grandpa causing a scene over the land."

"Well, you can't blame him. He was so proud of Pa for making such a success of the farm."

"And I'm the disappointment of the family."

She waved away his comment. "Don't be silly. Not one person thinks that. Anyway, let's not talk about it. I told Grandpa not to worry. But you know how he is."

"Yeah." Seth didn't fault his sister for opening up to their grandpa about his trouble with the mortgage and Luke's father's determination to buy Frank's land, which bordered Carson's. But he still had some details to work out, and he'd have preferred to let Grandpa in on the whole thing once he had things in hand.

Teddy puckered her brow as she looked him over. "By the way, why'd you get home so late? I expected to see you an hour ago."

"Let's go into the kitchen. Coffee smells good."

"It's just finished boiling. I figured you'd want something to warm your insides."

"You figured right." Seth followed her back to the kitchen and dropped into a chair at the table. He smiled his thanks when Teddy set a steaming mug of coffee in front of him, then took a seat across from him with a cup of her own.

"So," she said. "What kept you?"

Seth gathered a long, slow breath and released it along with the details of the past couple of hours.

"How sad for Rose that she never knew her sister wasn't the one returning those letters!" Teddy's eyes narrowed in anger. "And how dare that wretched aunt of theirs keep them apart." She spooned sugar into her cup with such force it splashed onto the table. "When I think about all the years our Rose mourned about her sister, I could just… It makes me so angry."

"It doesn't seem fair. That's for sure. I guess if Miss Potter and Rose had stayed connected all these years, we might have gotten to know her years ago."

And then the woman might have a better chance of tearing the children away from their home. If they'd grown up knowing her, they might even want to go live with her.

"How long will Miss Potter be staying in Prairie Chicken?" Teddy's question brought him back to the present.

He shrugged. "Not sure." Hopefully she would realize he wasn't going to budge about the children. She had seemed to accept his refusal to give them up, but Seth had a feeling it wasn't going to be that easy. He drained his cup and set it on the table. "Anyway, she's coming for dinner tomorrow night. That okay?"

Teddy's face lit up at the news. "Of course! I'll cook some deer steaks and put on a pot of beans with those little onions we dug up last month. This is wonderful."

A twinge of guilt hit Seth as he listened to Teddy. He supposed being the youngest by a good fifteen years and being doted on her whole life had given his little sister a naive view of people and their motives. He was about to tell her about Miss Potter's desire to raise the children herself, but he changed his mind as he watched Teddy continue to plan for the next evening's meal.

He only hoped Miss Potter wouldn't cause a scene and upset the children.

Ansley felt herself drawn to Teddy Dobson from the first moment she laid eyes on the young woman. If she had to guess, she'd say Teddy was no more than twenty. Still old enough to have married, but not so old she would be considered a spinster by any means.

"I'm so delighted to meet you," Teddy said, taking Ansley's cloak and hanging it on a hook by the door. "The girls have been so excited since they got up this morning, I'm sure Miss Vestal had a horrible time trying to keep their attention at school."

Ansley couldn't help but notice Teddy hadn't mentioned Jonah. Clearly, he'd made it known to this other aunt of his that he wasn't happy with Ansley's presence. He'd given her a dutiful kiss on the cheek when she arrived, no doubt instructed to do so by Mr. Dobson and Teddy. But the girls had milled about the instant she'd arrived, both talking at once. "I told everyone at school about you," Hannah said. "Sarah Wayne pretended she didn't care a thing about anyone having a new aunt, but I could tell she was envious. And Ma always said you shouldn't envy because it's a sin."

"I suppose that's right." Ansley grinned at the girl.

A tug on her dress brought Ansley's attention down to Lily. "I picked you some wildflowers at recess, but they made Miss Vestal sneeze so she asked me to take them outside. And then I couldn't find them after school."

Ansley bent and hugged the child, relishing the warm, plump arms that hugged her back. "Well, I appreciate the thought."

"Sarah Wayne said you'll probably be setting your cap for Uncle Seth," Hannah said, holding out a chair for Ansley and climbing into the chair beside her. "Think you might marry him?"

"I should say not!" Ansley instantly regretted the force of her words as the girl grew red and appeared as though she might start to cry. "It's just that I don't know your uncle, and besides, I'm not setting my cap for anyone."

Teddy clucked her tongue, but her eyes held a hint of merriment at the turn of conversation. "Sarah Wayne sneaks into those dime store romantic novels much too often. I've even seen her reading them at the general store. I don't know why her ma doesn't put a stop to it. They fill her head with the silliest ideas."

Seated at the head of the table, Seth grunted around a sip of coffee, but Ansley couldn't bring herself to meet his gaze. He set the cup on the table and turned to Teddy. "I've been meaning to speak with Miss Vestal about Sarah. It's one thing to fill her own head with silliness, but I don't want her talking about courting and marriage and such around our children."

Ansley couldn't help but agree that this Sarah Wayne seemed to be a source of trouble, but she knew his use of the term "our children" didn't include her. And she suspected he'd used it as a deliberate reminder that he considered Rose's children to be his, and he intended to keep it that way. Well, they'd just see about that.

"May I help you with dinner preparations, Miss Dobson?"

She shook her head and waved away the offer.

"You're a guest the first time you come to dinner. Next time you can help." Her smile was infectious and Ansley found herself smiling back. "And please call me Teddy. We're family now."

"Then you must call me Ansley." The young woman's smile widened, revealing a dimple in one cheek. All the tension Ansley had felt the day before about—Teddy's resistance to her taking the children faded. If she proceeded very carefully, she might just have found an ally. After all, a woman this young, pretty and bubbly surely must have a string of beaux dying to ask for her hand. Before long, she would likely marry. And if that were the case, Seth would have no one to help him care for the children. That circumstance might bode well for Ansley's desire to take the children back to Boston and raise them as her own.

As they laughed and talked around the dinner table for the next hour, Ansley felt a growing unease about her plans. Clearly, these children were loved, cared for and doted on by Mr. Dobson and Teddy. How would the children feel about leaving an aunt and uncle they had known their whole lives? Her mind drifted to the day Aunt Maude's lawyer came for her and Rose after their parents' deaths. They'd spent three months with the Cranes, a local family and good friends of their parents. Ansley and Rose had believed, as had the Cranes, that they would be adopted into the family. Leaving had felt cruel and unjust. And even if Aunt Maude had been kind, which she wasn't, they had resented being ripped away from a loving adoptive home.

Could she do that very thing to Rose's children? Would Rose have even wanted her to?

The thought nearly made Ansley cry, but she cleared her throat and gained her composure. Of course Rose would want her to raise her children. She refused to believe anything else. She couldn't let her growing affection for the Dobsons blind her to what must be done. One way or another.

She felt, rather than saw, Mr. Dobson's eyes on her. Turning her head, she met his steely gaze. Her stomach churned as he sipped his coffee, his eyes, never leaving hers. Finally, she couldn't bear it anymore and averted her gaze as Teddy regaled the children with stories of her three-day adventure in Martin's Creek, embellishing, Ansley felt sure, most of the details. The children clearly adored her.

Feeling suddenly out of place, Ansley stood so abruptly all the chatter ceased. "Are you okay, Auntie Ansley?" Hannah asked.

Her face warmed. "Of course. I just thought I'd start clearing the dishes for your aunt Teddy."

"Clearing the dishes is my job," Hannah said, and then she grinned. "But I'll share, if you want."

Seth gently tugged the girl's braid. "Nice try."

Slowly, Ansley sat back down.

"Besides," said Teddy. "Remember, the first time you're a guest. Next time you can help."

Slowly, Ansley lowered herself back to her chair. "I'll hold you to that."

"Are you coming to dinner again tomorrow night?" Jonah's question caused an awkward silence to fill the air. Especially since Ansley was pretty sure he asked the question not because he hoped she would, but because he hoped she wouldn't.

Obviously, Ansley couldn't answer. She hadn't been invited.

"Of course she is!" Teddy laughed out loud, a pleasant, infectious kind of laugh that included everyone in the room. "Good thinking, Jonah. And tomorrow I might just see how skilled our Ansley is in the fine art of dishing up rabbit stew. What do you children think? Shall we let her try?"

Her words set off a flurry of conversation from everyone at the table with not one, but two notable exceptions. Jonah sat, his arms folded across his chest staring at his empty plate. Forcing her gaze across the table, Ansley found Seth staring at her again. His eyes were hard as sapphires, his lips set in a firm line.

It was pretty clear his opinion of her mirrored their nephew's. He considered her to be the enemy, although he apparently hadn't said anything to Teddy about her real reason for continuing on in Prairie Chicken. Otherwise, the young woman would likely be giving her the same cold shoulder.

Ansley truly had no idea how long she would stay or what her plan would be. Still, she knew for certain that despite Seth Dobson's animosity, she would never, ever abandon her sister's children. And if she gained custody of the children, perhaps they could come back to Prairie Chicken during the summers. Her heart rose at the thought. Surely Mr. Dobson would see the generosity in such a plan. She would attend to their schooling, and he would get them each summer. If all went as planned, and these Dobsons weren't too difficult, perhaps they could find a way to share equally in the children's raising.

Chapter 4

Seth allowed Jonah to accompany him as he drove Miss Potter back to her boardinghouse. This served a twofold purpose. One, they'd be chaperoned, and two, he highly doubted she would be inclined to bring up the subject of taking over the children's care if the boy came along.

And his plan worked perfectly. The two-mile ride from the homestead to town was quiet. He'd have to talk to Jonah about his attitude toward Miss Potter, which, he was ashamed to admit, bordered on rude. Frank and Rose would never have allowed it. But tonight, the moroseness suited Seth's purposes.

They rolled into town and pulled up next to the boardinghouse after what seemed like hours. Miss Potter turned to Jonah. "Good night, Jonah," she said. "I hope we will become friends soon."

"Yes, ma'am."

Seth hopped down, walked around to her side of the wagon and helped her get down from the seat.

Accepting his gesture, she climbed from the wagon. "Thank you for your hospitality this evening, Mr. Dobson. I shall hire a wagon of my own and drive myself to your home for dinner tomorrow, so please do not trouble yourself with my charge."

Those words brought a frown to Seth's brow. Prairie Chicken was a friendly town, for the most part, but there were still scoundrels lurking about from time to time. And he couldn't allow a lady to come and go the two miles after dark. "It's no trouble, Miss Potter. I'd be obliged if you would allow me to fetch you home for supper."

"That is truly kind of you." She cast a quick glance at Jonah, who appeared to be all ears. When she turned back to face Seth, her smile wasn't quite sincere. "But I am quite capable of fetching myself."

Seth recognized the sound of stubbornness veiled in pleasantry. There would be no victory for him in this conversation. He offered her his arm. "Allow me to walk you to the door, at least."

"Of course." She slipped her gloved hand into the crook of his arm. "You know we must discuss the children's future." She kept her voice low as they walked, presumably to keep the conversation private.

"I'll never give them up," Seth said.

"A point you've made abundantly plain." She gave a sigh. "Clearly, Mr. Dobson, the children love you and Teddy. I could never take them completely from you. It wouldn't be fair. But will you consider the possibility that Rose would have wanted me in their lives, as well?"

Relief washed over Seth. Perhaps he wasn't going to be in for a fight, after all. Still, it was evident she wasn't giving up the children altogether. "What do you have in mind?"

She shrugged. "I'm not sure. But for every question there is an answer."

"I reckon we can put our heads together and try to figure it out. But I don't see how, with you living in Boston and us here in Kansas."

"Well, God would not have led me all the way across the country just to go home without a family to love."

Her impassioned words touched Seth's heart, but they scared him, too. Because from all indications she was right. God had allowed her to find them, but did that mean He intended for Jonah, Hannah and Lily to travel to Boston and live with Miss Potter? Guilt pricked at his fragile ego where the children were concerned. He hadn't always done the best by them—starting with their manners, as Mrs. Boatwright had pointed out earlier. And now they were in danger of losing the home their parents had built. Of course, no one had known Frank took out a mortgage on the farm. Frank had been the frivolous one of the family. And he always wanted to keep Rose in nice things so she wouldn't regret giving up her wealth for him.

He felt Miss Potter's hand on his arm and looked down into her kind eyes. "It is my hope to stay in Prairie Chicken until the end of the year so I can spend Christmas with the children. By then, perhaps we'll have figured out a way for us all to share in their raising, as I know my sister would have wanted."

The news that she was planning to stay for the next two months came as a surprise and raised Seth's suspicions further. What exactly were her intentions? She turned at the threshold. "Good night, Mr. Dobson. I'll see you tomorrow for dinner. Thank you again for the lovely evening."

Tipping his hat, Seth bid her good-night and turned to go.

"Mr. Dobson." The soft sound of Miss Potter's voice turned him back to face her. He waited for her to speak as she gathered a full breath. "You and your sister have done a remarkable job with Rose's children. Whatever may come of my presence here in regard to their future, please know I find nothing lacking in your abilities to raise them."

Seth pondered her words as he climbed into the wagon and flicked the reins. No doubt, she had meant to console him, but he couldn't seem to squash the ball of concern forming in his gut. Miss Potter clearly wasn't giving up the notion of taking the children to Boston.

Well, that would be over his dead body. He'd allowed himself to be taken in by a pretty face and wide, blue-green eyes for a minute. But the fact of the matter was, he'd promised his brother the children would be safe under his roof. That he would raise them as if they were his own, and nothing was going to convince him to go back on his word.

Ansley stepped into the bank the next morning. If she were to remain in Prairie Chicken for two months, she'd feel more comfortable depositing her funds in an account rather than keeping it all in the false bottom of her trunk.

The bank manager smiled a tentative greeting, then led her to a wooden desk. He motioned for her to sit across from him in a hard wooden chair, nothing like the plush, comfortable chairs in the large, elegant bank Ansley was accustomed to in Boston.

"What can I do for you?" he asked.

"I will be staying in Prairie Chicken until after the holidays and feel I must deposit my money for safekeeping." She presented him with several hundred dollars. His eyes widened and he sat up straighter in his chair.

"Why, yes, that is a fine idea." He pulled out a form and took the quill from his inkwell. He began to write. "I understand you came from Boston to see Mrs. Dobson." He glanced up. "I'm terribly sorry you had to come all this way to find out your sister is gone, Miss Potter," he said.

"Thank you, sir. Everyone has been very kind."

"I take it you've met the Dobson children, then?"

"Why, yes, on two occasions. And I am having dinner with them tonight, as well."

Pushing the document across his desk, he handed her the quill. "Please sign on that line."

Ansley did so and set the quill down.

Mr. Macomb glanced over the paper, shaking his head regretfully. "It's such a shame about Frank's farm."

Though clearly the little inchworm was trying to manipulate her for some reason, Ansley frowned and allowed herself to take the bait. "I'm sure I don't know what you mean."

Looking down, he fidgeted with his glasses, wiping the lenses with his handkerchief. "Oh, heavens. I just assumed Seth would have spoken to you about it, considering you're as much those children's family as he is."

"Mr. Macomb, perhaps you'd better just tell me whatever it is you think I should know." She leveled a gaze at him.

His eyebrows rose, then he shoved the spectacles back on his nose and clasped his hands together atop his desk. "The fact of the matter is that Frank Dobson took out a mortgage on the farm. Seth has been working not only his farm, but also whatever extra work he can find to stay on top of things, but he's fallen behind by two full payments. In another week I shall have no choice but to foreclose."

The news seized her stomach. Mr. Dobson certainly didn't seem like the sort of person to shirk responsibility. But then the banker hadn't said he was behind on his own mortgage, but rather one he had inherited. Her heart went out to him at the thought that he had to work so hard to try to keep from losing Frank and Rose's land—the children's inheritance.

"Mr. Macomb, you don't seem all that sorry, if you ask me."

He shrugged. "I'm a businessman, Miss Potter. And while I don't smile on the misfortunes of others, the sale of the farm would bring in a sizable sum for the bank."

"How much is owed on the mortgage?"

He named a ridiculously small sum. Still enough she'd have to have her attorney send her a bank draft.

"I shall make arrangements to pay the mortgage in full. In the meantime, you may take the two payments we are behind from the account I am opening and apply them immediately."

"Certainly, Miss Potter. I'll attend to that this afternoon and send your receipt to the boardinghouse."

Aunt Maude had not raised a fool. Ansley shook her head and plastered her most pleasing smile on her face. "Mr. Macomb, I do not intend to leave the bank without a receipt. Now, I truly do not want to squander my time sitting here until this afternoon. So if you don't mind, I'd appreciate if you would apply the payments immediately and make out my receipt."

In an instant, his face grew red. He cleared his

throat and stood. "Of course," he said, his tone tight. He scooped up the stack of bills she had placed on his desk and headed toward the door. "I'll see to it."

He returned within moments. "There now. Your account is set up in your name, and the mortgage is now current and out of danger."

Ansley stood and took the receipt. "Thank you, Mr. Macomb. Now, if you wouldn't mind keeping this between us, I would be grateful."

Walking in step with her as she made her way to the door, the banker frowned. "You are suggesting I lie to Seth?"

"Of course not. But perhaps if he asks about it, you might just say an anonymous benefactor has settled the debt. I will certainly tell him eventually, but I would prefer he not hear about my involvement from another source."

He hedged just for another beat, then nodded. "I'll do as you ask."

Ansley stuffed the receipt into her reticule and slipped it around her wrist.

"Thank you for your help, Mr. Macomb. Have a good day."

He opened the door for her and stepped back.

Aunt Maude always said don't reveal your hand too soon. The fact was she could see two outcomes once Mr. Dobson discovered what she'd done. On one hand he might be grateful and be more willing to talk sensibly about the children's future. But on the other hand, if he felt she had somehow provided charity, he might be more difficult.

She stepped into a cool, sunny fall morning and turned toward the livery, where she intended to rent a wagon and horse for the duration of her stay.

"Miss Potter!"

She turned at the sound of her name echoing across the empty street. She cringed at the sight of Luke Carson hurrying toward her. Planting a smile on her lips she braced herself. "Good morning, Mr. Carson."

"Mornin'. I was hoping I'd run into you."

"Oh? What can I do for you?"

He swiped his battered hat from his head and smoothed his hair across his forehead. "Well, fact is, there's sort of this fall dance at the schoolhouse on Saturday. And since I heard you're staying in town through Christmas, I thought you might let me escort you."

Dread filled her. Propriety demanded a polite answer, something that didn't reveal her revulsion. But there was simply no circumstance that would convince her to accept this vile man's invitation.

"You honor me, Mr. Carson."

His face brightened and Ansley hurried on before he got the wrong idea. "But I'm afraid I will have to decline."

As quickly as he perked up, his face fell. He twisted his hat between his large hands. "I reckon you do."

Ansley's heart clenched in her chest. Reaching out, she touched his arm. "Perhaps, if I attend, you might ask me to dance?"

A slow grin spread across his face.

"Sure. I'd be proud to."

"Well, good day, then, and perhaps I'll see you there."

"Miss Potter?"

With a sigh she turned back to him.

"Boardinghouse is thataway." He jerked his thumb in the opposite direction she was heading.

"Yes, I'm headed to the livery to rent a horse."

"Oh, well then, I'll just walk with you. If I know

Mr. Watson, he'll try to swindle a pretty little gal like yourself."

"I assure you, Mr. Carson, I am not the sort of woman to be swindled."

His eyes showed his disappointment. "Oh, well, you mind if I was to walk you anyhow?"

That was the last thing she wanted. But since she'd just refused his invitation to the dance, Ansley couldn't bring herself to decline his attempt at chivalry.

"All right, then. But I'll do my own negotiating with Mr. Watson."

Mr. Carson rattled on as they walked, but Ansley's thoughts drifted to the upcoming dance.

It had been ages since she'd had any fun. Would Mr. Dobson ask her to dance? She couldn't help the image floating through her mind. Resting in his strong arms as he turned her around the dance floor. A smile tipped her lips as she walked inside the livery.

Chapter 5

"What do you mean they're already gone?" Seth frowned at the station manager, demanding to know what had happened to Miss Potter's things. Unable to sleep the night before, he'd had a sudden twinge of guilt at the thought of Frank's sister-in-law doing without her trunks or having to pay someone to fetch them. After all, she was almost family, and Frank would have set out two days ago to pick them up. Seth had left the house at 3:30 to get there by first light, slushing through the muddy, rutted road for fifteen miles, only to discover the trunks weren't there.

Frustration hit him hard and he slapped his hat against his thigh. "Who picked them up?"

The station manager shrugged. "A man stopped by. He said Miss Potter hired him to deliver her trunks to Prairie Chicken." He waved a thick hand toward the crowded restaurant. "I got customers, mister. Between the train passengers and stagecoach stops, I ain't got time to worry about one woman's trunks. You want the truth? I was glad to get rid of them. They was in the way."

Seth knew Ansley hadn't commissioned anyone. She'd told him the night before she hadn't done so yet. "So you just give anyone's things away without checking a man's story?"

The burly man scowled and puffed his cigar. "Mister, you accusing me of something?"

Seth eyed him. He doubted he packed the same punch as this man, but he was at least fifty pounds lighter and most likely twice as fast. He stood his ground. "Only incompetence."

Clearly realizing Seth wouldn't be intimidated, the station manager tossed his cigar to the ground and backed away. "If a person pays the fee and says he's here to pick up trunks or whatnot, I give him the goods. Plain and simple. Now, you got yourself a beef with that, feel free to write a letter to Mr. Malone, who owns this station. Otherwise, I have things to do."

"Fine. Can you at least describe the man to me?" The last thing he was going to do was let some scoundrel steal those trunks away from Miss Potter.

"Dark hair, kinda tall. I don't know. That's all I remember. I wasn't trying to paint the fella's portrait. Now, like I said. I got work to do."

Dog-tired and wrestling with the idea that he might not be able to recover the trunks for Miss Potter, he turned his wagon around and headed out of town the way he'd come. He'd hardly slept all night long, thinking about Miss Potter's obvious desire to steal the children from him. Well, stealing might be a bit strong a word for what she hoped to accomplish, but the end result would be the same if she succeeded. Would she take him before a judge? The woman was wealthy. That much was clear. She could afford a whole slew of lawyers. Would she bribe a judge to rule in her favor? She didn't seem the sort to stoop to something like that, but you couldn't always tell about a person. And she wanted her sister's children badly.

He'd also considered her assurance that she didn't want to take the children away from him and Teddy. But even so, it was clear she wanted to be a part of their upbringing, too. Seth could never agree to the children being carted from Boston to Kansas for equal time between them, so if that was her plan, she could just forget it. He'd mortgage his home to the hilt to fight her in the courts.

Five miles outside of Martin's Creek, Seth noted a wagon stopped at the side of the road. He frowned as he approached. A man had climbed into the back of the wagon and appeared to be rummaging through a large trunk…one such as Miss Potter might have stored at the stage station. He pulled up alongside the wagon and greeted a stranger. He fit the station manager's description: tall, dark hair. The trunk's contents were scattered along the wagon bed—mainly women's clothing and a few books. How dare he? He pulled on the reins and wrapped them around the brake. The man stood to his full height in the wagon bed. Seth met his steady gaze. "Those trunks wouldn't happen to belong to a Miss Potter, would they?"

The other man eyed him, his hand going slowly to the gun hanging from the belt at his hips. "As a matter of fact, they do."

"Mind telling me why you're riffling through a lady's private things?"

The man's eyebrows went up and his hand gripped the handle of his pistol. "Mind telling me why that's any of your business?"

"It so happens Miss Potter is the sister of my late brother's wife. I went to the station to pick up her things only to discover they were gone. Now, what I'd like to know is why you have them. And why you're going through them."

The man took his hand from his gun. "I suppose it does look a bit suspicious." He offered a wry grin that Seth didn't believe for a minute. "But there's an explanation."

"I'm listening." Seth folded his arms across his chest.

"I rode into Prairie Chicken on the stage with Miss Potter. She bemoaned being forced to leave the trunks behind so I decided to do the gentlemanly thing and retrieve them for her."

Seth couldn't imagine Miss Potter bemoaning anything, especially the inconvenience of being forced to leave a couple of trunks behind. But he would give the man the benefit of the doubt…at least until he got the rest of the explanation. "Why are the trunks opened and her things lying all over the wagon bed?"

A rueful smile twisted the man's lips. "Turns out I don't handle a team all that well. The wagon hit a rut and the trunk fell out of the wagon and broke the lock. It just opened on its own and spilled the contents." He grabbed an unmentionable from behind a wheel and winked at Seth as though sharing a private joke at Miss Potter's expense.

Seth bristled at the blatant lack of respect. Besides, he knew this fellow was lying. "Well, let's get her things back in the trunks and I'll take them off your hands."

"That won't be necessary." Dropping all pretense, the man's voice went cold. "I like to finish what I start."

Not a good answer. "You'll either hand over Miss Potter's trunks, or I'll go to the sheriff and report this. As far as I know, stealing a person's luggage is a crime."

The man narrowed his eyes. But Seth wasn't the sort of man to be intimidated by a thief and a scoundrel. And clearly, this man recognized that he was in for a fight if he didn't give up those trunks. He raised his palms and let his arms drop. They slapped against his thighs. "That won't be necessary. It's not worth losing time on a frivolous errand to the sheriff's office. Besides, it's your word against mine. And my story is reasonable, don't you think, Mr. Dobson?" He dropped the article of clothing into the trunk and rested his hand on the butt of his gun at his side.

"How did you know my name?"

"Kinda hard to live in Prairie Chicken for more than a day and not know who Seth Dobson is. You have a lot of friends."

"If you live in Prairie Chicken, how come I've never seen you before?" Seth kept a close eye on the man as he jumped down from the wagon. He stayed back with legs planted, in case the other man lunged.

"As I said, I came in on the stagecoach a few days ago. With Miss Potter, as a matter of fact. I'll be honest, Mr. Dobson, I was pretty taken with her. I thought picking up her trunks for her might convince her to allow me to come calling."

The man's lies just kept coming, but Seth didn't bother to call him on this new one. As he'd said, it was his word against Seth's. And the explanation did seem reasonable. He might have believed it himself if he hadn't caught the thief going through Miss Potter's things.

Seth tensed as the other man stepped forward. Then relaxed as the fellow offered his hand. "My name's Mitch."

Seth couldn't trust a man who didn't offer his last name, but he shook his hand nonetheless.

Mitch picked up a couple of books from the ground. "Must've missed these." He tossed them into the trunk. "Tell you what," he said. "I'll help you load these trunks into your wagon, and you give me your word this is just between the two of us."

Seth leveled his gaze at the thief. "Just between the two of us? Give me a good reason I shouldn't warn Miss Potter to stay away from you. Furthermore, I'm still not convinced I shouldn't go to the sheriff about this."

"Look, I work for Mr. Carson. It's hard enough to be a stranger in town without having this unsubstantiated rumor following me around making folks all suspicious."

"You're Carson's new man?"

"That's right."

"Mitch what?"

"Lane."

"Well, Mr. Lane. I'll take the trunks off your hands. I won't be going to the sheriff for now."

"Sounds fair." He turned and grabbed one of the trunks. True to his word, he loaded it into Seth's wagon. Seth loaded the other, still keeping his eye on Mitch.

"So this is just between us? I'd hate for Miss Potter to think I've been rummaging about in her trunks."

"But you have been."

"No. I was simply putting her things back." He tossed a grin. "Why do I get the feeling you don't believe the trunk came open on its own?"

"I'm not one to call a man an out-and-out liar."

"So our agreement stands?"

"For now."

Something about Mitch Lane made him uneasy. He knew almost certainly he had been looking for something in that trunk. He didn't seem like a petty thief, but looks were, more often than not, deceiving. If he couldn't trust his eyes, he'd have to follow his instincts.

At twilight, Ansley climbed into the saddle and nudged her new horse forward. Originally, she'd planned to rent a wagon, but she'd quickly found herself unable to control a team. Horseback just seemed wiser. And the price of renting a horse for two months was nearly the same as purchasing this one, so she now owned the mare and had named her Bella. When she left town, she could leave the mare with the Dobsons, or if things went as planned and the children went with her, she could ship the horse to Boston for one of them. Perhaps even Jonah. Maybe the boy would soften toward her by then, and if not, surely his own horse would…

Her face flushed at her thoughts. Imagine trying to buy the boy's love with a horse. She was as bad as Aunt Maude offering to send Rose abroad for a year after she learned of her "friendship" with Frank Dobson.

Enjoying the glorious brushstrokes of red and pink in the sky, Ansley gathered in a clean, full breath and relished the sound of Bella's hooves rustling up the fallen leaves. As much as she missed the bustle of Boston, Ansley had to admit there was a charm and peace that came from slowing down and enjoying the scenery, the feeling that no one was rushing, annoyed, or asking her to move aside. Perhaps this had been why Rose's last few years had been so satisfying.

Just outside of town, Ansley met up with Mr. Dobson. He pulled the reins and halted his wagon. "Good evening, Miss Potter." He touched his hat, and the setting sun glinted off his blue, blue eyes.

"Good evening to you, too, Mr. Dobson. Didn't we discuss my transportation to your home?"

He nodded. "We did. But I picked up your trunks today and thought I'd kill two birds with one stone."

"Oh, how thoughtful." Ansley smiled. "I'd planned to hire someone today, but found myself once again preoccupied with other little errands." She cringed at her own words. What if he did the polite thing and asked about those errands?

"Well, now there's no need. Here they are all safe and sound."

Ansley noted the smudges beneath his eyes, the weary rise and fall of his shoulders. It struck her that he would have been riding in the wagon most of the day to have driven thirty miles round trip. The gesture tugged at her heart. "That must have been a great deal of trouble."

"No trouble at all."

"You must allow me to compensate you for your time." As soon as she made the offer, Ansley saw it was a mistake. He frowned.

"That isn't necessary or desired, Miss Potter." His voice held a chill, and she knew without doubt she'd offended him deeply.

"I meant no insult, Mr. Dobson, but since I had intended to hire someone..." And perhaps he could use the extra funds, considering what she'd learned at the bank this morning.

"Family does not accept payment from family."

"Well, we aren't really family."

He expelled a breath. "Close enough."

Ansley chided herself inwardly. Why must she always get the last word? "Again, I apologize."

"Apology accepted," he said. "Now, shall we go back to the boardinghouse and unload these trunks?"

"Yes, please. I am sure Mrs. Boatwright will have no objection to your carrying them upstairs, given the circumstances." Ansley wasn't entirely convinced of the truth of her words. But the proprietress had gone out for the evening, so she wouldn't be there to object anyway.

Honestly, all the rules Mrs. Boatwright inflicted on her residents were so restrictive, it was a wonder she had anyone living there at all. Besides Ansley, Mrs. Boatwright and Alice's family, there were two elderly women, Miss Vestal and the sheriff, who wasn't there very often. None of those folks seemed stifled by the rules, but Ansley had lived most of her life controlled by her aunt and mostly confined to a musty old mansion. She wasn't sure she could bear two months of Mrs. Boatwright's rules.

Ansley pulled the horse around and nudged the animal into a canter as they headed back to the boardinghouse. They rode in silence; she, embarrassed at having offered him money, and he… Ansley couldn't be sure what was on Seth's mind but she could imagine he was insulted and angered by her offer. She should have known better. Of course a proud man like Seth Dobson wouldn't accept money. But couldn't he understand that where she came from, and with her resources, it was rare to offer payment and have it refused?

Should she try to make her case to Seth or leave well enough alone? She gave a little sigh and chose the latter. After all, to remind him of her wealth would only reinforce his opinion of her. And heaven help her when he discovered what she had done at the bank this morning.

At the boardinghouse, she stood helplessly as Seth muscled the first trunk onto his shoulder. "Lead the way," he said. She hurried up the steps, breathless by the time she reached her room. She opened the door and hung back in the hall so as not to offend Mrs. Boatwright's sense of propriety.

"What do you have in these things? Rocks?"

"I'm sorry. They are quite heavy. It took two men to load them on the train. You must be very strong."

He gave her a lopsided grin that made her heart pick up. "Maybe I'm just more determined."

Ansley couldn't help but return his smile, impressed and a little surprised by his humility.

"Where do you want it?" Seth asked, his breath labored.

"Anywhere is fine."

Ansley headed back downstairs and outside to the wagon before Seth had set the trunk down. A glance inside the wagon bed revealed the other trunk. Something didn't seem quite right. She looked closer. When she saw the problem, she gasped. The latch had been compromised. Ansley pressed her hand flat on her stomach. Had Seth gone through her things?

"I apologize for the state of your other trunk." The sound of his voice turned her toward him. "It fell hard against the side of the wagon. The roads are bad after the rain yesterday."

"I see."

He ducked his head as he moved around her and reached for the trunk. "Several items fell out, I'm afraid."

Ansley gasped as she thought about the breakable items in the false bottom.

Seth cleared his throat. "I'll just take this up and set it next to the other one."

"Thank you." She reached out, and then pulled her hand back. "Please, be careful."

Ansley mounted her horse and waited for Seth to emerge from the boardinghouse.

"Sure you don't want to leave your horse and ride in the wagon? I'm going to see you home later anyway."

Honestly, the man was so stubborn…" Well, I suppose there's no point in riding then."

Seth nodded. "Sensible." He unwrapped Bella's reins from the hitching post. "I'll just get her bedded down in the barn. Won't take a minute."

"May I accompany you?" Her cheeks grew warm.

Seth jerked his head around to meet her gaze. Ansley hurried on to explain. "Mr. Watson explained what I must do to care for her, but it would be helpful to watch the process."

A wry grin tipped the corners of his mouth. "You mean to tell me you bought a horse without knowing how to take care of it? Even Lily knows how to do that."

The thought of that tiny girl scooping up hay and wandering that close to the massive animal sent a wave of fear to Ansley's stomach. "Isn't that dangerous for a child Lily's size?"

"Don't worry, all she does is feed the chickens. But she does know how to take care of the horses."

Clearly, his implication was that if a five-year-old could do it, a woman her age certainly should have the knowledge.

His ungentlemanly reference to her age raised her defenses. "Well, our horses are boarded at the stables. We live in the city after all. So the care and grooming of livestock wasn't part of my education."

"Hey, no need to get riled up."

"I am not riled up." She stomped ahead of him.

As Seth unsaddled Bella, he handed Ansley the saddlebag. "There's something in there."

"Oh! I would have forgotten." Reaching inside, she pulled out the gifts she'd purchased earlier. "For the children."

"Gifts?" He scowled. "We try not to spoil them."

"I see." Ansley glanced down at the gifts. "Maybe I should take them back to my room, then. I—I don't have children. I just thought...well, these are simple ribbons for the girls and this...maybe you're right." The gift for Jonah was not as small and simple. She'd seen a bone-handled knife and bought it. But what if Seth and Teddy thought she was trying to buy his affection? And was she trying to do just that?

"Miss Dobson...Ansley." Seth's eyes were kind and his expression softer than she'd seen thus far. "I'm sure the children will be grateful. And maybe it's not so much spoiling them, coming from you, since you're not the one raising them."

Ansley peered closer at Seth, weighing his words. Had he meant to make her feel better about the gifts, or was he telling her plain and simple that she wasn't the children's guardian and never would be?

Chapter 6

Seth had to admit he was enjoying the evening more than he'd thought he would. Miss Potter's humility and willingness to put the gifts away until after supper had been a good start to the evening.

Jonah's behavior toward Ansley was beginning to annoy him. The boy had barely said two words to his aunt during supper. While Seth figured Ansley was hoping her gift would soften the boy, he could have told her these children couldn't be bought. At least that's what he was counting on. He sat at the head of the table, sipping coffee and watching his family laugh over pie.

He caught Ansley's gaze and her silky eyebrows rose in question. He grinned and nodded. At least she was still deferring to his place as the children's guardian.

"Everyone listen," Seth said. "Your aunt Ansley has something for you."

The children turned to her. Ansley's face flushed as she stood and walked over to the counter where she'd set the packages earlier. The children had cast curious glances throughout dinner, but not one of them had asked about them.

Ansley handed a package to each of the three children. "It's not much, really. I just thought you might like these."

The girls oohed and ahhed over the ribbons. But Jonah made no move to unwrap his. He glanced at Ansley. "No, thank you."

"Oh, I'm sorry, Jonah. I just thought…" Her voice broke around her words. "Perhaps you're right."

Seth snatched up the package and clapped Jonah on the shoulder. "Come with me."

"Oh, Mr. Dobson, please…"

Ignoring Ansley's protest, he marched Jonah outside, onto the porch.

"Now, what was that all about?" he demanded.

Jonah looked down at his scuffed boots and shrugged.

"Look at me," Seth said. Slowly, the boy lifted his stormy gaze to Seth's. "Now, explain yourself."

"I don't want nothing from her."

"Well, that's too bad. You think your ma would have wanted you to be rude to her only sister?"

"She didn't love Ma. She never answered her letters or came to see her. Ma cried sometimes."

Drawing in a deep breath, Seth released some of his anger. "Jonah, the truth is your aunt Ansley didn't know about the letters. She didn't even know where your ma lived."

A frown creased Jonah's brow, but he didn't respond.

"Your ma and Aunt Ansley lived with their aunt. And she was angry with your ma for leaving Boston and marrying your pa, so she had the letters sent back without Aunt Ansley ever knowing anything about them."

Jonah looked down again, kicking at the wood planks beneath his feet. "You think that's true?"

"From what I've seen of your aunt, I do believe her. She's grieving her sister, just as much as you're grieving your ma and pa. But you can't take it out on her." He shoved the package toward the boy. "You do what you think is best, but whether you keep the gift or not, you owe her an apology."

Seth walked back inside, leaving the boy to mull over his words.

"Did you give him a lickin', Uncle Seth?" Lily's sad eyes met his.

"No, just a good talking to."

Ansley's breath left her in a whoosh and he realized she'd been wondering the same thing.

Teddy set a slice of pie in front of him. "Where's Jonah?"

"Doing some thinking. He'll be back in soon."

Teddy jabbed her hands on her hips and glanced around the table. "Come on, girls, let's clean up, then we'll have a story before bed."

Ansley stood. "Since this is my second time here, I am no longer a guest," she reminded Teddy. "I get to help."

Teddy grinned. "Okay, another pair of hands will make things go a lot faster."

By the time the women finished cleaning up, a very subdued Jonah came back inside. In one hand, he held the empty paper and in the other, his gift.

Ansley remained where she sat, her eyes thoughtful and waiting, as they observed Jonah. He went straight to her and sat in the chair next to hers. "I reckon I gotta say I'm sorry for the way I've been acting."

"Oh, Jonah, I understand."

He shook his head. "I didn't know you never got Ma's letters. Just thought you didn't care."

"If I'd known where she was, I'd have answered every one of them. I might even have come to see you all from time to time."

"That would've been good."

Lily, unable to sit still another second, sat up on her knees and flung herself across the table. "What'd you get, Jonah?"

Snatching up the girl, Teddy gave her a little swat on the rump. "Silly girl. You know better than to get on the table."

"Well, I want to see Jonah's present."

A slow grin spread across Jonah's face and he held up the very knife he'd been eyeing at the general store for the past six months.

A sickening churning started in Seth's stomach as Teddy's eyes went wide and she glanced at Seth. "That's beautiful, Jonah!"

He nodded. "It's the one I been wanting." He turned to Ansley and threw his arms around her. "Thank you."

"You are most welcome." Ansley's face beamed with pleasure as she held Jonah for the brief time the boy allowed.

Seth forced a smile, but as he looked at the bone-handled knife, he thought about how easily Ansley Potter had strolled in, dropped some cash like it was nothing and purchased the very item Teddy had been saving egg money to purchase for the boy's Christmas present.

Was that how it would be if she decided to fight him for custody?

Unable to take it anymore Seth shoved to his feet,

mumbled an excuse about chores and stomped out into the crisp fall night.

Pain swelled inside his chest at the very thought of the children leaving him. He knew he had to at least consider Carson's offer to buy Frank's land. It was the only way he could fight if Miss Potter decided to pursue custody. And even if he lost in the end, at least they would know that he gave everything he had to keep them.

Ansley stepped into the telegraph office the next morning, hoping to find a reply from her lawyer. She could still feel Jonah's warm body in her arms and reveled in the memory. The more time she spent with the children, the more convinced she was that she was doing the right thing. She shoved aside the thought that they might resent her for tearing them away from Seth and Teddy. That she was trying to do the same thing Aunt Maude had done to her and Rose.

But it wasn't the same thing at all. This wasn't selfishness. She wanted the children because she believed she could give them a better life than they might have here in Prairie Chicken.

Five minutes later, she walked back onto the boardwalk, disappointed that there was no answer from her lawyer.

Ill at ease, she walked slowly, nodding hello to the other residents on the street. Women in homespun and rag bonnets, all pressed and clean. They smiled but didn't offer to stop and chat. Loneliness called out to her, a sense that she didn't belong here. She could be a visitor, but she simply wasn't one of them.

There were no plans for her to see the children that day or evening, and she felt a sense of loss as she contemplated what to do with her evening. When she arrived back at the boardinghouse, she stepped past the porch and went around back to the barn. On a whim, she saddled Bella, taking care to cinch the straps tight enough without hurting the animal.

She climbed into the saddle and headed off in the only direction she knew to go. Toward Seth and Teddy's home. The day was sunny. With no rain the day before, the ground had hardened so she gave Bella her head and allowed her to trot along the rutted road.

There was no one home when she reached the Dobson's house. Disappointment flooded her. She'd looked forward to a chat with Teddy. She started to head back to town when an idea came to her. Turning Bella she continued down the road. Teddy had told her Frank and Rose had lived just a few miles away.

Ansley's heartbeat quickened as she rode the distance to the cabin where Rose had made her home. She almost felt guilty, like a thief about to sneak into a home when the owners were away. Only the sound of leaves rustling beneath Bella's hooves provided any break in the silence.

Finally, she saw a cabin sitting alone in the clearing. No smoke curled out from the chimney, even on this cool morning, so Ansley knew she'd found the right place. The barn and cabin looked cared for, as though someone came periodically to make sure it didn't become run-down. The thought that Seth and Teddy would keep up the cabin pleased Ansley. They truly were good people.

She dismounted and wrapped Bella's reins around the post that stretched across the porch. Taking the one step up, she jumped as the sound of her heels on the wooden porch startled her.

Tears sprang to her eyes. She wished like anything

she could open the door and Rose would be on the other side, baking bread, offering her a cup of tea. If she'd known where Rose was, they might have had mornings like that during Ansley's visits.

Well, there was nothing to do but go on inside or get back on Bella and head to the boardinghouse. She hesitated only a second longer and turned the latch. Shoving the door open, she stepped inside. Other than the thick layer of dust covering every surface, the cabin had clearly not been disturbed since Frank's and Rose's deaths. On one side of the room sat a beautiful settee with roses and leaves, and a wooden rocking chair. The fireplace was against the far wall between the living area and kitchen. Clearly, Frank had built Rose a lovely home and had given in to her desire for lovely things. Even Seth's two-story farmhouse didn't have such lovely furniture.

In the kitchen, the pots and pans were not of general-store quality. These resembled the ones used by Aunt Maude's cooks. Ansley knew they were expensive, as Aunt Maude gave the cook a sound tongue lashing once when she burned a hole in the pot and it had to be replaced.

She brushed her fingertips along the sleek top of the table. Where Seth and Teddy's table was clearly handmade, this one also looked store-bought.

Walking into the bedroom, she found a tidy, lovely little room with a bed, wardrobe, and an oak desk in the corner. She walked to the desk, curious about the papers, but didn't feel comfortable riffling through any of it. Of course, it made no sense to leave all this just sitting here. Someone would have to go through their things and begin packing it all away either to give away to charity, or store for the children for when they were older.

With a sigh, she walked back into the living area, only to be greeted by a low growl. She gasped and stopped short at the sight of an enormous, furry beast of a dog. She knew she had two choices. She could either do a quick step back into the bedroom, close the door and hide until the dog went away, or she could try to make the animal trust her.

Forcing a pleasant tone, she reached out a shaky hand. "Hello there, boy…or girl. It's okay. You don't want to bite poor Ansley, do you?"

The dog stopped growling and tilted its head to one side, as though trying to figure out what on earth she was talking about. Encouraged, Ansley took a step forward. The dog followed suit, until eventually, they met in the middle. Ansley stood, unsure what to do next. If she tried to pet the animal, would she lose some fingers? Before she could decide, the dog gave a quick bark and jumped, resting his massive paws on her chest, nearly knocking her off her feet. Terror seized her as she stepped back to avoid losing her balance. Just as she was about to scream for help, the dog's pink tongue stretched out and left a wet stream from her chin to her forehead—including her nose.

He dropped down, turning in circles at her feet, his tail knocking against the rocking chair, settee and table. Ansley wiped her face with her sleeve and let out a nervous laugh. "Well, I'm glad you were only bluffing," she said. "But how on earth did you get inside?"

"The latch is tricky. If you don't know how to shut it just right, the door comes open."

Ansley jerked around at the sound of a man's voice to find Seth standing in the doorway, pistol drawn, looking formidable.

"Goodness, Seth, you nearly scared me to death."

There wasn't a hint of apology in his eyes as he looked from her to the dog—which he clearly dismissed as a nonthreat—and back to her. "What are you doing here, Ansley?"

Ansley shrugged and absently scratched the dog's head. "I wanted to see where Rose lived."

"We would've been happy to show you the cabin if you'd asked."

How dare he imply she was intruding.

Seth opened the door wider and called the dog, who went to him easily. He shooed the animal outside and closed the door behind it.

"I did stop at the house. There was no one home."

A frown creased his brow as he slipped his gun back into the holster on his hips. "Oh, that's right, Teddy was going to take a meal to one of the older women.

"So you see?"

"I guess you probably think Rose lived beneath her station, don't you?" He waved to include the entire room.

"Actually, I was surprised to find that she had such nice things. Even the boardinghouse doesn't hold a candle to the furnishings in this little cabin."

A sigh left Seth and he nodded. "Frank wanted her to live the way she was accustomed to living."

"Are you saying my sister was the cause of Frank's living beyond his means?"

His gaze shifted quickly from the furnishings to meet hers. "What do you mean they lived beyond their means?"

Caught, Ansley inwardly chided herself. "I just… well, it seems as though perhaps a farmer couldn't afford these things. But I haven't been here. So I couldn't possibly know."

"Well, Frank always was a little fancy for his own good. And it wasn't Rose's fault he lived above his means. He just wanted to give her things."

"He must have loved her very much."

Seth nodded. "He did. Are you finished here, Miss Potter? I'd be happy to escort you back to town."

Obviously she was being dismissed. Ansley nodded. "There's no need to escort me to the boardinghouse," she said. "I'd hate to pull you away from your own work." She smiled to show him she wasn't just being stubborn. But she had almost revealed her place in saving the farm and she was afraid if they continued the conversation about Frank's frivolous nature, she might divulge the information before she was ready.

Outside, they said their farewells. Then Seth turned back to her. "Miss Potter?"

"Yes?"

"There is a harvest dance in town tomorrow night. Would you like to go?"

Heat rose to her cheeks, and her heart sped up. "I'd love to, Mr. Dobson."

He nodded. "Teddy thought you might. We'll stop by the boardinghouse and pick you up on our way. You probably won't want to ride Bella to a dance."

"Thank you."

He touched his hat. "We'll see you then. Have a good day."

Her excitement plunged. Of course he wasn't inviting her as a beau. She was such a fool.

Chapter 7

An hour after leaving Ansley, Seth sat across from Mr. Carson. The man did not appear to be wealthy, though the whole town knew he had more money in his bank account than the rest of the residents of Prairie Chicken combined. "Well?" Mr. Carson asked, lacing his fingers atop the oak desk. "Do we have a deal?"

Seth knew he had the option to keep his late brother's land in the family as a legacy for the children. While the two girls would likely marry and move into a home built by their husbands, Jonah very well might want to live in the home his parents had shared, where he'd been born. The decision weighed heavily on Seth's mind. The amount Mr. Carson was offering for the land adjoining his was above market price. The proceeds would secure the children's future.

For the past month, he'd been trying to make a decision about Mr. Carson's offer. Still, he had come to the agreed-upon meeting today with no idea what Frank would have wanted him to do.

"I'm waiting, Mr. Dobson." The tapping of Mr. Carson's fingers atop his desk grated on Seth's nerves like the sound of a wagon wheel in need of a good greasing.

"Your offer is generous, Mr. Carson."

"I'd say more than generous."

"Okay. More than generous." Seth pushed the unsigned document across the desk. "I'm just not ready to commit to the sale."

Annoyance passed over Mr. Carson's face. He grabbed the document and rolled it up, then continued his tapping with the document. "Really, Seth. You've had months to think it over."

"And I appreciate your patience." Seth refused to allow this man to intimidate him.

"You've misinterpreted my interest in your brother's land as patience, and you're testing my goodwill." He set the paper down and leaned back in his chair, scrutinizing Seth, his fingers steepled in front of his substantial stomach. "I know your brother's land was mortgaged. And according to my sources, you're two months behind."

Anger hit Seth's gut like a sucker punch. His sources? Who but the bank officer had known about the mortgage? He stood, resting his fists on the desk. "Look here, Mr. Carson. It's true the land is mortgaged and I'm two months behind. But it's also true there are only four payments left."

Seth would not allow Mr. Carson to swoop in and steal the children's inheritance before he could make good on the loan.

He stared at Carson, hoping he had hit a nerve, but the man's eyes betrayed nothing. He stood, meeting

Seth's gaze head-on. "You have until tomorrow to sell the land I'm requesting, or I have it on good authority your brother's land will be for sale by the bank. I'm doing you a favor by trying to give you a fair deal before that happens."

The blood drained from Seth's face. He knew Carson was a snake—who in Prairie Chicken didn't? But it hadn't occurred to Seth that he himself might get bitten. "Rex knows I'm good for the money. He's agreed to wait two more weeks, so your threats don't hold water, Mr. Carson."

A short laugh found its way through the older man's lips. "As I said, you have twenty-four hours to see reason. The price I'm offering is more than fair. Or would you prefer to be the reason those poor children grow up penniless? Is that what your brother would have wanted?"

Though he had been inclined to consider Mr. Carson's offer just in case he needed it to fight for custody of the children, now Seth knew he'd never give the man one acre. "I wouldn't sell you my brother's land at any price." He jammed his hat onto his head. "And you can take that to the bank."

His hands started shaking the second he mounted Brewster and didn't stop until he made it home—after an unsettling visit with Rex Macomb, the bank manager.

Teddy poured him a cup of strong, steaming coffee and sat across from him. She waited until he'd swallowed his first sip before questioning him. "Whatever is the matter?"

"Carson is forcing me to sell the land to him by tomorrow."

"Forcing? But how can he?"

He shrugged. "If we don't sell to him by tomorrow, he'll let the foreclosure go through and get the property from the bank. You know he's only offering the higher price because of how he felt about Ma."

Rolling her eyes, Teddy scowled. "Imagine him being sweet on her all his life—poor Mrs. Carson."

"Well, we can be thankful for his feelings if it helps us get more out of the land." He sighed and slapped the table. For all of his resolve, Carson had him over a barrel. "I don't see that we have any choice."

Teddy averted her gaze and bit the inside of her lip—a sure sign she was plotting something.

"What are you thinking?"

She looked him square in the eye. "I'll tell you, but you're not going to like it."

"Go ahead. Whatever you have to say can't possibly be any worse than our other two options."

"Ansley."

"What about her?" Seth lifted the cup to his mouth and took another drink.

"Well, she has lots of money—part of which belongs to Rose, or would if Rose were still alive. I bet you anything she planned to put away Rose's share for the children."

"What does that have to do with Frank's land?"

"Jonah's and Hannah's and Lily's land, you mean."

He shrugged and conceded the point. "Okay. What does Rose's inheritance have to do with the children's land?"

Teddy sent him a scowl that would have broken a weaker man. "Seth Dobson, your head is so thick sometimes it's a wonder you can button your own shirt. What I'm suggesting is speaking to Ansley about paying the mortgage so Rex can't foreclose and Mr. Carson can't swindle us out of it."

"You mean to tell me you want me to go to that woman and give her a reason to lord it over us? If we ask her to pay off the mortgage, she'll have proof we're not fit to raise Frank's children, Teddy. She'll snatch them up and ship them off to Boston before we can say 'boo,' and you know it."

She set her chin in stubborn defiance. "I think you're wrong. I don't believe Ansley would take them away, and I believe she will help if she can."

"You can forget it, Teddy. I won't beg her for money."

Teddy opened her mouth to protest more, but Seth stood, nearly knocking his chair over. He stomped across the room.

"You're being pigheaded, Seth."

Yanking open the door, he glared at his sister. "Maybe so, but I'm not going to speak to Miss Potter about the mortgage, and that's the end of the matter."

For as many mornings as she'd awakened in Prairie Chicken, Ansley's sleep had been interrupted by the sound of Alice's children. Children playing, children crying, children running up and down the steps, children laughing—each time followed by the sound of their mother's insistent shushing. Ansley didn't fault them. Of course children must move about, and it must be trying for their mother to raise them in one room of a boardinghouse. But Ansley's generosity didn't help her sleep any better, and after five repeatedly interrupted nights, she feared she must be looking as haggard as she felt.

She was just finishing her morning routine when a knock sounded on her door. A glance at her watch brought on a groan. For all Mrs. Boatwright's warning, Ansley just had not been able to drag herself down to breakfast. Each morning Mrs. Boatwright had grudgingly brought a breakfast tray, although she threatened each would be her last.

"Come in, Mrs. Boatwright," she called, securing one last hairpin in place.

The door opened. "I'm not Mrs. Boatwright, but may I still come in?" Teddy had opened the door a crack and stuck her head in, her smile brightening the room.

Ansley stood and welcomed Teddy with a hug. "Of course. I'm delighted to see you." She motioned toward a wooden chair in the corner of the room. "It's not very comfortable, I'm afraid."

Waving away her apology, Teddy sat resting her reticule on her lap. "It's fine."

"What brings you here this morning? Are the children all right?"

Teddy's fingers twisted around the lace string of her bag, and her usual happy demeanor seemed to be missing. If nothing was wrong with the children, then it must be something else. Because she wasn't acting like herself. "Teddy? What's wrong?"

"Seth is going to be furious with me for coming." She caught Ansley's gaze. "There's a problem, Ansley. A big problem I think only you can solve."

Ansley listened intently while Teddy poured out the details of Seth's dealings with Mr. Carson and the bank. The girl was nearly in tears by the time she finished her outrageous story. Ansley stood abruptly and went to her desk."

"Teddy. Mr. Carson has been misinformed about the status of the mortgage."

A frown creased Teddy's brow. "What do you mean?"

Ansley lifted the receipts for the mortgage payments. She handed them to Teddy. The other woman glanced at them, then back to Ansley, confusion clouding her eyes. "I'm not sure what it is you're showing me."

"Those receipts prove the mortgage is up to date."

Understanding slowly dawned and Teddy's eyes went wide. "You mean you already knew about it?"

"Mr. Macomb informed me of the situation. Although I'm still not sure if he did it on purpose or by mistake. Either way, I paid the mortgage payments and I have ordered a bank draft to pay off the rest. It should be here in a few days."

"I just don't know what to say, Ansley!" Teddy shot to her feet and threw herself into Ansley's arms. "Oh, oh, oh…what are we going to tell Seth?"

Chapter 8

Anger burned Seth to his core as he stalked out of the bank and swung himself into Brewster's saddle. Well, anger and relief, but mostly anger. How dare those women go behind his back like that? Teddy's betrayal hurt the most. After a night of fitful sleep, he'd decided all he could do for the children was sell the land above asking price to Mr. Carson rather than let the bank take it back and leave them with nothing.

He'd met with Carson at the bank, but Rex Macomb—the little worm—had twisted his delicate white hands together and stuttered through the explanation. The bank no longer had the right to foreclose on the property, as Miss Potter had settled the debt. The only satisfying part about the meeting was Carson's stormy eyes and red face. Seth wouldn't want to be Rex when Carson got through with him.

Who did Miss Potter think she was to go to the

bank and settle an account for him? She should have come to him first. Even if Teddy had instigated the whole thing.

He rode at breakneck speed to the boardinghouse only to discover Teddy and Miss Potter had left an hour earlier. "They went to Frank's cabin," Mrs. Boatwright said quietly. "Ansley's decided to move in until she goes back to Boston, so they went out to take a look at the place and have a picnic with the children."

"I should have known." Seth's boots hit the floor with heavy thuds as he walked back to the door.

Mrs. Boatwright followed. "I don't know what put a burr in your saddle, Seth, but Ansley moving into that cabin is just sensible—although she is paid up here for another week. You know my policy about refunds. Anyways, you'd best simmer down and have a chat with the Lord before you hightail it in there and say something you'll regret."

"Believe me, I won't regret a thing, Mrs. Boatwright."

She shook her head, disappointment evident in her downturned lips and the deep frown creasing her brow. "I've never known you to be a cruel man, Seth Dobson. Ansley has as much right to that cabin as you have."

Seth nodded his acknowledgment and stepped into the crisp late morning air. As much as he tried to ignore the guilt tensing his gut, he couldn't get Mrs. Boatwright's words out of his head. By the time he reached the cabin five miles outside of Prairie Chicken, he had cooled down quite a bit. Enough that he could at least confront the women rationally.

At the cabin, he reined in Brewster, hopped down and wrapped the reins around the porch rail, and then stepped inside.

Teddy was standing next to the fireplace, attempting

to ignite some kindling. She jerked around and gasped. "Now, Seth, don't overreact."

"Overreact?" He kept his voice even. "Just because my own flesh and blood went behind my back and did exactly what I forbade her to do?"

Her lips twisted in a wry grin that grated on Seth's nerves even before she spoke. "Honestly. Betrayal? You're not overreacting a bit. Besides, I am not your daughter. I'm your sister. I do whatever I choose to do. Oh, why won't this fire start!"

Seth stepped to the fireplace and gently nudged her out of the way. "Let me do it."

"You be nice to Ansley, Seth. I mean it. Things aren't as they appear."

Seth carefully blew on the struggling fire and watched, satisfied, as the flames licked up through the kindling. "There," he said, and added the larger wood. "It should warm up in here soon." He stood and faced his sister once more. "I told you I would handle the situation without involving Miss Potter. Where is she anyway?"

"The children took her down to show her the creek."

He glowered down at his sister once more. "Why did you do it?"

Teddy's responding grin ignited his wrath even more. "Now you're laughing at me?"

"Oh, Seth. Calm down. No one is laughing at you. The fact is I did go over to the boardinghouse to speak with Ansley today. When I explained the situation, she showed me the receipts for the mortgage payments. And the fact is she has contacted her bank in Boston to send a draft to pay the rest of the mortgage."

"I suppose that's why she believes she has the right to move in here."

"No, she has the right because she is Rose's sister."

"And she has the right to pay off the mortgage without even telling us?"

"She did it to save the children's home. And considering how you're acting, can you blame her for keeping it to herself?"

"I was taking care of things." Still smarting, Seth couldn't quite let it go.

Teddy placed her hand on his arm. "Don't you think the children would rather have their home than the money it would bring?"

Seth steeled his heart against the emotion welling inside of him. "They have a home…with us."

"Now you're just being bullheaded." Teddy walked to a crate on the floor. She lifted a cloth from the crate and headed to the table where a bowl of water sat. She dipped the cloth and began to wipe away the dust. "Do you know they come here sometimes?"

Seth drew in a quick breath. "Alone?"

She turned and looked him square in the eye. "Together."

"I had no idea."

"I care as much about the children's welfare as you do, Seth. Besides, you aren't being fair to Ansley. Just because she is wealthy doesn't mean she's greedy. She loved her sister and even you have to admit she loves the children."

"But she doesn't even know them. Not like we do." She hadn't stayed up with them at night, wiped their tears those first few weeks after their parents' deaths, bathed them, dressed them, prayed with them, fed them. What right did Miss Potter have to swoop down and try to steal them away?

"She's here now, and it's not fair to judge her. She spent all those years not knowing where Rose was or that she even had children. You need to give her the benefit of the doubt and stop being so suspicious of her motives."

"Well, maybe I know a little more than you do."

She turned back to face him, her eyebrow raised. "What are you trying to say?"

It was time to let his little sister in on all the facts. Perhaps then she wouldn't defend Miss Potter's motives quite so much. "It so happens Miss Potter has already made it pretty clear she wants to take over the children's raising." He paused. "In Boston."

Rolling her eyes, Teddy gave another wave of her hand, completely dismissing his revelation. "Is that all?"

"Is that all? It doesn't bother you that she waltzes into town and thinks she can raise them better than we can?"

"It doesn't worry me in the least. And of course she wants to raise them. Can you imagine the wonderful education they could get back east? Not to mention everything money can buy. If I were in her position, I'd want the exact same thing. And I might not be nearly as nice as Ansley has been."

Shock burst through Seth, and he stared at Teddy. Did he even know the young woman standing before him? "You mean to say you think we should just give them up to Miss Potter?"

"Of course not. And if you give Ansley half a chance, I can almost guarantee that by Christmas, she will be in full agreement that they should be raised right here in Prairie Chicken."

As usual, Teddy was being far too trusting. "Maybe, but I doubt it," Seth said.

Ansley dressed with special care that night. She wasn't sure what to expect from Seth. She and the children had returned from the creek earlier that day to see him riding away.

She finished dressing early and went downstairs to wait in the parlor for them to arrive. Mrs. Boatwright joined her. "You did the right thing, Ansley. Seth's just stubborn."

The last thing Ansley wanted to do was discuss the situation with this woman. "He's not stubborn. He has been working very hard to keep the children's inheritance secure. I think he's to be commended."

"Well, of course. Seth is the best man I've ever known." She paused and Ansley could feel her scrutiny. "It seems as though you are beginning to see what a good man he is, too."

"Of course."

The bell above the door signaled someone's arrival, much to Ansley's relief.

Mrs. Boatwright grinned. "That's going to be for you."

Seth stood in the foyer as Ansley and Mrs. Boatwright walked out of the parlor. Ansley caught her breath. He wore a black suit and his hair had been freshly barbered and combed neatly away from his face.

"Good evening," he said. His eyes moved over her, then the hard look returned. Clearly, he was still angry with her.

"You look very handsome, Mr. Dobson. Shall we go?"

He stepped forward and offered her his arm.

After saying good evening to Mrs. Boatwright, they ventured out into the cold night air. Seth offered her his hand as she climbed into the wagon.

"Where are Teddy and the children?" she asked as he took the driver's seat.

"Already at the school. I dropped them off first."

Ansley drew in a deep breath and released it with her words. "Go ahead and get it over with."

"Get what over with?"

She faced him, folding her arms across her chest. "Clearly you're upset. Teddy said you would be."

"If I am upset, as you say, it is simply because you went to the bank without consulting me."

"First of all, I didn't go to the bank to take care of the mortgage. I was simply there to open a bank account. But what was I to do when Mr. Macomb confided that Frank's farm was in jeopardy?"

"You could have come to me before you paid it."

"And what would you have said if I had *consulted* you?" Anger started to build in her. "Teddy made it pretty clear you were against my involvement in the first place. Besides, if the issue were about your farm, of course I would have come to you rather than pay it on the spot. But this was my sister's home. Her children's inheritance. I felt I had no choice."

"Do you also feel you have no choice but to move into the cabin?"

Refusing to be baited, Ansley shook her head. "I'm just being frugal."

"And since you paid the payments you believe you have the right."

Honestly, he was being insufferable. "I don't have any rights, but my sister would have welcomed me into her home."

"You're right, Ansley. I shouldn't have said that."

She reached inside her reticule and pulled out the receipts. She handed them to him. "These belong to you and as soon as the draft comes through, I will hand over the deed, as well."

The school yard was filled with wagons and horses

as they approached, and Seth pulled on the reins. He wrapped the leather straps around the brake and hopped down. Ansley would have liked nothing more than to help herself out of that wagon before he could reach her, but to even try would be folly, so she sat until he offered her his hand.

"Miss Potter…Ansley, I know you thought you were doing what was best. But I've been caring for the children for months now. I don't need your help to give them a good future. Even if I had been forced to sell the land, the children will inherit my property."

"And what happens if you get married and have children of your own? Will they still inherit equally?"

His lips twisted in a wry grin as he offered her his arm. "Trust me, Miss Potter, I have no intention of ever getting married. But if by some chance there is a woman out there suited to me, then of course I would never put any children born to me above those three."

Clearly, he believed he'd yet to meet his future bride—which meant he certainly didn't consider her courting material. Ansley was glad for the cover of night as heat moved up her neck and into her cheeks. Was he thinking that she was implying he should marry her?

They walked into the school, which was filled with music, as several musicians had already begun to play at the front of the room. Couples were already beginning to take the floor. "May I take your cloak?" Seth asked.

She shrugged out of it and handed it to him. "Thank you, Mr. Dobson."

"I'll go put this up and be right back."

She watched him go and wondered if he would ask her to dance when he returned. Feeling a tap on her shoulder, she turned to find Luke Carson grinning at her. "Well, here I am, asking you to dance like you suggested."

There was nothing to do but accept his invitation. "Thank you, Mr. Carson. You do me a great honor."

As he clumsily took her in his arms, Ansley caught sight of Seth headed back to where she'd been standing. When he saw she was gone, he looked onto the dance floor and found her. The quick scowl that marred his face lifted Ansley's spirits quite a lot. She smiled at Luke, suddenly wondering if perhaps Seth might think of her as courting material after all.

Chapter 9

Seth spent the day cutting trees and splitting wood, enough to last a while for both his household and the cabin. He might not be happy about Ansley moving into the cabin, but he couldn't let her freeze to death.

He walked into his cold, dark house after six, irritated that Teddy had decided to have her dinner with Ansley. He washed up and warmed the meal of leftover deer roast and fried potatoes with green beans boiled in pork fat. He had to admit it was still tasty, even if he'd eaten the exact same thing last evening.

Not that they hadn't invited him. Teddy assured him Ansley had requested he join them for dinner, but he insisted he needed to build up the woodpile. Which was only half the truth. The other half was that even a week later he was still smarting over Ansley paying off the deed. Although as the days wore on, he was growing less and less defensive about her actions and was starting to see his reaction as one of excessive pride. Instead of being grateful she had saved the cabin, he had taken it as an insult. The thought made him squirm a little on the inside. He'd behaved badly and Ansley deserved an apology, which he should have offered days ago.

After he did his chores, Seth paced the floor and glanced at the clock, impatiently waiting for eight to arrive. He had agreed to pick up Teddy and the children from the boardinghouse then. If tomorrow hadn't been Saturday, he'd never have agreed to let the children spend the evening there.

At seven, he could stand it no longer. He grabbed his coat and hat and hitched up the team. When he reached the boardinghouse, he didn't bother to knock. The only time the door was locked was between eight each night and five each morning. He headed toward the sound of laughter coming from the library.

Hannah's voice rose above the laughter. "Maybe we can stay all night with you sometime."

Lily chimed in before Ansley could answer. "Then you could tuck us in and tell us more stories about when Mama was a little girl."

A sense of helplessness hit Seth swiftly and full in the gut. Clearly the girls already preferred their new aunt to him and Teddy. Well…to him, anyway. Would they want to go and stay with Ansley while she was in the cabin?

He stepped inside the room. Ansley glanced up and smiled. His heart tripped inside his chest. Ever since the dance last week, he had been a ball of conflict. One minute he wanted Ansley to board the train and leave Prairie Chicken forever. The next, he wanted to take her hand and go for a long moonlit walk with her, listening to her soft, low tones as she spoke about her life. Past and present.

Teddy broke into his musings. "You're early, brother-dear."

"I missed my family." Seth dropped into a wing chair and Lily crawled into his lap.

"We ate chicken. And Mrs. King made a scrumptious pie." She grinned her gap toothed, dimpled grin. "Apple."

"You and your love of apple pie." Seth couldn't hold back a laugh and he tickled his niece's stomach. She giggled.

"The children were just saying how happy they are that Ansley is moving into the cabin." Teddy smiled at him, daring him to say something about it.

"We want to spend the night in our old loft." Hannah's voice rose with excitement. "Can we, Uncle Seth?"

Seth met Ansley's gaze and noted she was holding her breath. "If it's okay with your aunt Ansley, it's okay with me."

Ansley's breath left her as her eyebrows rose and a slow smile lifted the corners of her full lips. "That would be lovely."

Teddy rose from the sofa and gathered up the children. "Time to go. Say goodbye to Aunt Ansley."

They protested, of course, but Ansley stood by Teddy and promised she would see them soon.

Seth hung back as Teddy moved the children toward the door. Ansley turned to him. "I didn't ask the children to spend the night with me."

"I know. I heard them ask." Seth smiled, trying to set her at ease. "I wanted to apologize for the way I acted last week. I know it wasn't your intention to waltz in and try to take over. What I should have done was thank you for helping to save the children's farm." He finished, out of breath, and waited for her response.

She gave him what could only be described as an affectionate smile. The same smile he had seen her bestow upon the children. While he'd much rather receive the sort of smile a woman gives a man, at least she wasn't frowning. "Mr. Dobson, thank you for saying that. I just want to enjoy the time I have left in Prairie Chicken. The children deserve to have us getting along, don't you think?" She held out her hand. "Truce?"

Seth couldn't hold back a grin as he took her proffered hand. "Truce."

The next morning, Ansley awoke early and packed her meager things. She wanted to be ready to go when Seth arrived to load the trunks in his wagon and drive her out to the cabin. Her stomach tripped over at the thought of going to live in the cabin. She'd never lived alone and she wasn't sure she could take care of herself. But mostly she was excited about the new adventure. After years and years of caring for Aunt Maude according to the old lady's whims, then living with staff who refused to make any changes to their routine and finally enduring Mrs. Boatwright's rigid rules for the past two weeks, she was more than ready to do whatever she wanted in her own home.

A knock at her door pulled her from her reverie. "Come in."

Mrs. Boatwright entered, carrying an envelope. "This came for you. Telegram."

Ansley's heart picked up rhythm as she took the envelope.

Mrs. Boatwright hesitated, her eyes narrowing. "I

thought maybe you'd given up the idea of taking the children away."

Ansley gasped. "Did you read my telegram, Mrs. Boatwright?"

"Of course not, girl. You can see plainly the envelope is sealed."

"Oh, you're right." Ansley reached out and touched her arm. "I'm sorry. I'm just a ball of nerves today."

"So I take it that telegram is going to be in response to the one you sent last week?"

Ansley shrugged. "I don't know. It could be from anyone." And she certainly wasn't going to read it with Mrs. Boatwright looking over her shoulder.

"Well, along with the telegram, I came to tell you Seth is here. He's drinking coffee in the restaurant. Said for you to take your time."

"Thank you, Mrs. Boatwright."

She nodded and reached for the door. "You could do worse than Seth Dobson, you know."

Of all the intrusions! "I'm sure I don't know what you mean."

Clearly undaunted by Ansley's obvious offense, Mrs. Boatwright continued her diatribe. "And I'm sure you do. I've seen the way you look at him. And quite frankly, I've seen the way he looks at you, too. Instead of trying to take those children, why don't you try nurturing whatever is between you and Seth. You two get married. It's like killing two birds with one stone."

"Mrs. Boatwright..."

The elderly woman raised her palm. "All right. I'll mind my own business. Come down when you're ready and I'll let Seth up here to pick up the trunks."

"Thank you."

Mrs. Boatwright left, closing the door behind her.

Hands trembling, Ansley opened the envelope. *Hearing in Martins Creek, Kansas* STOP *January 4* STOP *Traveling Judge* STOP *Defendant will be notified by mail STOP*

Dread hit her full in the stomach. She hadn't intended for him to file with the courts, only explain her rights under the law.

Perhaps Mrs. Boatwright had a point. What if she pursued the custody agreement and lost the chance for a lifetime of love and family with not only the children, but Seth, as well?

She shook her head at the thought. She was no romantic schoolgirl like Sarah Wayne reading dime novels. She certainly wasn't going to abandon her efforts to gain custody on the off chance that she might find love.

Stuffing the telegram inside her reticule, she grabbed the small bag that she'd carried with her onto the stagecoach, which was large enough for only one gown and her underthings.

When she stepped inside the restaurant, Seth lifted his arm and waved her over. Guilt nearly overwhelmed her stomach and as she reached his table, it was all she could do not to break down and confess. "Would you like a cup of coffee?"

She shook her head.

He frowned. "Everything okay? You're looking a little peaked."

"Just a little tired." She smiled, trying to convince him of her words so he would let the matter drop. Otherwise, she might spill the entire truth here and now and ruin all the progress she'd made with him.

Mrs. Boatwright approached the table as Seth was pulling out a coin for his coffee. "Oh, keep it," she said, waving away his payment. "You ready to come upstairs and get Ansley's trunks?"

Fifteen minutes later, Seth offered Ansley his hand and helped her into the wagon. Bella was tethered to the back of the wagon, her saddle next to Ansley's trunks.

"Thank you for taking the trouble to do this for me," Ansley said.

"It's my pleasure, as long as you stay put now. I don't know how many times I want to carry those boulders in and out of my wagon." He laughed as he said it.

"I promise to stay put." She only hoped he would still want her to stay in the cabin once he discovered that the legal process had begun for her to get custody of the children.

Halfway to the cabin, a horse and rider came toward them. Ansley felt Seth tense. Ansley recognized the rider as a fellow passenger on the stagecoach from Martin's Creek, the man who had not introduced himself. She'd later learned his name was Mitch Lane. She had to admit he looked rather dashing astride his horse, his suit free of dust and wrinkles. He stopped his horse as Seth pulled on the reins to halt the wagon. It would have been rude not to do so.

Mitch tipped his black hat and grinned at Ansley. "Miss Potter. It's nice to see you. I trust you've settled in since your arrival."

"Actually, she's just getting settled in today, so if you'll excuse us..."

Ansley frowned at Seth's rudeness. What could he possibly have against this man, who had only come to town two weeks ago? Of course, Ansley had thought Mr. Lane was ill mannered when he climbed out of the stagecoach before the ladies. But his manners seemed perfectly acceptable today.

"It is lovely to see you again, Mr. Lane." Ansley knew her voice was just a little sweeter than normal, her smile a little brighter. But she felt compelled to make up for Seth's rudeness.

"And you, too, Miss Potter. I'm glad to see your trunks arrived." He motioned toward the back of the wagon.

How thoughtful of him to remember. "Yes, thank you. Mr. Dobson was kind enough to travel to Martin's Creek and retrieve them for me."

"Ah, how good of Mr. Dobson," Mr. Lane said.

"Well," Seth said. "We're trying to beat the rain."

Once again, Ansley failed to understand his surliness. It was almost as though...well, surely Seth wasn't jealous of Mr. Lane's attention toward her. Her stomach dipped at the thought, and then just as suddenly, she chided herself for being foolish. Two handsome men were not going to fight over a twenty-nine-year-old spinster—not unless they were after her money. Another ridiculous thought. Seth had already been pretty clear how he felt about her wealth, and Mr. Lane couldn't possibly know she was an heiress.

"Of course. I wouldn't want Miss Potter to get rained on." Mr. Lane smiled at Ansley and touched his hat. "I hope to see you again soon, Miss."

Ansley's face warmed. Perhaps Mr. Lane had an interest in her after all. Seth Dobson certainly didn't. "Thank you, sir. I'll look forward to it. Perhaps at church tomorrow?"

"Perhaps." He nodded his farewell to Seth and nudged his horse. It was all Ansley could do not to turn and watch him ride away.

Seth flipped the reins and the wagon lurched forward once again. "You need to stay away from Mitch Lane."

A gasp filled Ansley's lungs. How dare he? "I don't see how it's your business."

"I have reason to believe his intentions aren't exactly what they seem."

"I'm sure I don't know what you mean."

"Don't be a fool. Mitch Lane works for Mr. Carson, the man who tried to steal your sister's home out from under her children. And now he's suddenly behaving like a suitor?"

"I see. So only a fool would believe a handsome man like Mr. Lane might possibly want to court someone like me?" Her voice broke as she fought back angry tears.

"Now, look here, that's not what I…"

"It's of no consequence, Mr. Dobson. And I refuse to discuss it any further."

He shrugged. "Suit yourself."

Ansley folded her arms across her chest. "Thank you. I will."

They rode the rest of the way in silence. When they reached the cabin, Ansley didn't wait for his assistance, but instead she climbed quickly from the wagon while Seth set the brake. She strode to the cabin and opened the door.

"Welcome home!" Teddy and the children greeted her.

"Look, Auntie Ansley," Hannah said, pointing to the wall. "We made signs for you."

Lily took her hand and led her to the table. "See? I picked flowers." Someone had set a pitcher of autumn wildflowers in the center of the table. Reaching down, Ansley pulled the five-year-old into her arms. "You children did this for me?"

"Aunt Teddy helped," Hannah said.

"Only a little," Teddy said. "The children did most of it themselves."

Lily wrapped her chubby arms around Ansley's neck and whispered in her ear. "I wish you could marry Uncle Seth and we could all live here."

"Lily!" Clearly the girl's loud whisper had carried. Teddy scowled at the child.

Over Lily's shoulder, Teddy grinned and rolled her eyes at Ansley.

"Besides," Hannah piped up. "If Uncle Seth married Aunt Ansley, we'd all live in Uncle Seth's house."

"We would not!" Lily's tone was outraged at the very thought.

"Girls," Teddy admonished. "That's enough."

"But Aunt Teddy, Hannah told a big fat lie. You know she did."

Ansley's face burned as they continued the conversation around her. She turned and found Jonah by the fireplace. The boy had grabbed the poker and stoked up the fire. She walked across the room. "Thank you. Maybe you could show me how to start the thing."

"You don't know how to build a fire?" The boy's surprise did nothing to alleviate Ansley's embarrassment.

"I'm afraid not. We have servants to do that for us."

"You have servants? I thought the war set them all free."

Ansley laughed. "Well, mercy, Jonah, I don't have slaves. My servants are mostly Irish men and women and I pay them a salary to work for me."

He frowned. "You pay someone to build your fires?"

The whole conversation was beginning to become comical. Especially now that the girls had stopped arguing and were listening with interest. Ansley glanced at Teddy, who was trying hard not to laugh.

"Yes, there are seven fireplaces in my home, and yes, I do pay a man to build them. He also takes care of the grounds."

"What are the grounds, Aunt Ansley?"

"Why..." Ansley stared at Hannah, not quite understanding the question. Then she realized. The children didn't have a yard with gardens and bushes and trees except for the woods surrounding the cabin. She smiled to include all three curious children. "The grounds is the acre my house sits upon. It is up to my groundskeeper to keep the flowers healthy and the bushes clipped and even."

Jonah nodded. "What do you do with the grounds?"

The question was a valid one. After all, every piece of land had a purpose on a farm. There were fields of wheat and corn, vegetable gardens. Suddenly her life seemed very frivolous indeed.

Thankfully, Seth entered, lugging her trunk through the door.

Lily was the first to greet him. "Look, Uncle Seth. We made signs and I picked flowers."

"That was thoughtful of you." Seth's breath came in bursts as he struggled with the heavy trunk.

Hannah hopped in front of him. "And Aunt Ansley has servants who light all seven of her fireplaces and make sure her flowers are pretty."

Seth laughed, despite the burden he carried. "I can imagine she does."

"Children," Teddy said. "Let Uncle Seth through."

"Where do you want this?"

"Anywhere is fine."

He seemed relieved as he set the trunk in the middle

of the sitting room floor. His gaze found Jonah. "Want to help bring in the rest of Aunt Ansley's things?"

"Yes, sir." Jonah hurried across the room.

In minutes, the wagon was unloaded. Seth stood at the door, his hat in his hands. He motioned to the children. "Let's go."

"Can't we stay?" Hannah asked. "Aunt Ansley needs our help. We can walk home later."

Seth shook his head. "It's raining, so you can't walk today."

"Well, Aunt Ansley said we could stay some nights."

"I'm sure she didn't mean her first night."

Normally, Ansley would have followed Seth's lead, since it was obvious he didn't want the children to stay. But the thought of being alone was weighing more and more heavily on her mind the closer the time came for the family to leave. "I'd love for them to stay."

Seth sent her a scowl and addressed the children. "You don't have your church clothes."

Teddy smiled. "I'd be happy to come back over and bring them."

Seth caught Ansley's gaze, his hazel eyes perusing her face, searching. "You don't want to be alone tonight, do you?"

She shook her head, and averted her gaze, feeling like a total fool.

"Okay. They can stay."

Ansley caught her breath and looked up in surprise as the girls threw their arms around Seth.

Seth glanced at Jonah. "You staying here or coming home?"

Ansley held her breath as he shrugged. "I think I best stay, Uncle Seth. She don't know how to build a fire.

The girls'll freeze to death if I don't keep it going." He seemed downright proud.

Seth nodded, pride and perhaps some amusement, shining in his eyes. "I think you're probably right. Maybe you should teach her how to build a fire in the morning. After all, you can't stay here every night."

Ansley accepted his comment for what it was—a reminder the children belonged with him. Her mind went to the telegram in her reticule and she forced herself to hold his gaze.

"We'll be by in the morning to fetch all of you for church."

Teddy gave Ansley a quick, tight hug. "I'll bring their clothes over in a little while." She pointed to the counters. "We brought over a few supplies to get you started. I can take you to town next week with the wagon so you can get stocked up. Most of us have already bought our supplies for the winter, so Mr. Dennis at the general store might have to order this and that, but if you run out of anything while you're waiting, you know where we are."

Ansley smiled. "Thank you. I appreciate it."

"You're welcome." She walked to the door, and then spun around. "I almost forgot. There's a cold cellar next to the cabin with butter and eggs and some meat. And down the path out back there's a smokehouse. Seth brought over some bacon and ham. There are some cuts of beef, as well. So you should be all set for meat."

Overwhelmed by their generosity, Ansley could only thank her. She stood on the porch, protected from the rain by the eaves hanging over the porch. The children joined her, and Lily slipped one chubby hand into hers. Hannah stood on her other side and did the same.

Ansley's heart nearly burst from her chest, and she could imagine Rose's joy that she and the children were building a relationship.

Now if only Seth would understand. How long before he learned of the upcoming lawsuit? And when he did, would she see the children again?

Chapter 10

By morning, Saturday's cold rain had turned into four inches of snow on the ground. And there didn't seem to be an end in sight as the snow fell, wet and heavy. Seth shook the snow from his boots, and then pulled them off as he came into the house from morning chores. He hung his coat on the peg next to the door and walked into the kitchen. Teddy stood at the stove, fixing breakfast.

"Sit down and warm yourself," she said. "I'll get your coffee. Breakfast is almost ready."

"Thank you." He padded to the table in stocking feet.

"Seems strange not having the children underfoot, doesn't it?" She poured the steaming hot coffee into his cup, then moved back to the stove and turned the bacon in the pan.

"I guess I better hitch up the sleigh after breakfast and go get them."

Teddy lifted slices of bacon onto a plate and cracked

open two eggs in the skillet. "I've been wondering if you would, or if maybe you'd consider letting Ansley have another day and night with them."

Seth frowned at his sister. "Without any word?"

"The children know what to expect during this kind of weather. They'd probably be surprised if you did show up over there." A shrug lifted her shoulders as she slid a spatula under the eggs and flipped them over. "I took the children clothes so they'll be fine there. And I added a few more supplies since they were staying the night. Even with three more mouths to feed, they should be cozy with more than enough."

Seth stared at the plate she set in front of him, but his mind followed the image Teddy's words had conjured. Ansley and the three children snuggled up together laughing, reading, singing, all in the cabin where the children longed to be in the first place. Of course they longed to be there with their parents, but was their mother's sister the next best thing?

Teddy sat and nibbled on a biscuit, her steady gaze on him. Seth glanced at her. "That all you're eating?"

Grinning she nodded. "No need to be a good example today. The children aren't here."

He sipped his coffee, watching her over the rim of his cup. Perhaps it wasn't fair to Teddy that they'd been forced to care for Frank's children. She had barely turned twenty years old when they came to live here. But she had taken over their care so naturally, it had never occurred to Seth that she might be giving up a chance for her own life, husband, family, by taking on the role of mother to three children. "You probably need a day off, don't you?"

Averting her gaze, Teddy stared at her cup, fingering the rim with her forefinger. "I have to admit, it might be nice to sit in front of the fireplace with a cup of coffee and just stare in silence for a while. The house is rarely silent anymore." She glanced up and met his gaze. "Not that I'm sorry you took the kids. Not at all."

Seth believed her. But guilt still wound its way through his heart. "Whatever happened to that fella in Martin's Creek, used to come courting every so often?"

Teddy's cheeks bloomed. "Billy?" She gave a nonchalant wave of her hand. "He took up with a girl closer to home. Grandpa was fit to be tied. I thought he might go after him with his shotgun."

"Have you given more thought to going to live with Grandpa?"

Teddy had been all set to move to Martin's Creek to keep an eye on their paternal grandfather just before the accident.

"You know I'd never leave you to take care of the children alone. We're in this together. I'm an old maid and you're an old bachelor and the children need us."

"I never intended for you to give up your life to help me raise them. Things are smoothing out around here, now that the children are getting used to living here. Maybe we need to start thinking about getting you moved to Grandpa's after all."

A frown creased her brow, but not before Seth saw something akin to hope flash in her eyes. "I couldn't do that to you or the children." She grinned. "Besides, it sounds like you're trying to get rid of me. Should I be insulted?"

Seth chuckled. "No, but you should consider the idea."

Her expression sobered. "I'll think about it and pray. But I can't imagine God would send me away when I'm needed here." She swallowed down another bite of her biscuit. "Too bad Grandpa is so stubborn. If he'd sell out at Martin's Creek and move here, it would solve everyone's problem."

Seth knew exactly why their grandfather refused to do that. Teddy would never be free to find her own life if she was wrapped up taking care of three children, an old man and Seth. He had to figure out a way to set her free.

Ansley sipped her coffee and watched the snow falling outside the window. She was used to winter snows and had always loved to watch the falling flakes, but she had never seen the beauty of evergreens laden with snow. The wooded trees beyond the cabin were, branch after branch, covered in white—the exquisite beauty reminded her of a painting. Still, despite the beauty, she knew danger lurked for anyone caught outside very far from home. She would not be venturing out to services.

The children had stayed up well past bedtime, curled up next to her in front of the fireplace while she told stories of her childhood with Rose. They wanted to hear all about living in a big house and more about the strange idea of her having servants. Their amusement made her laugh, but also she started to consider how ridiculous it was for a woman alone to live in a house the size of Aunt Maude's. Even if the children were to come live with her, the very real idea had begun to form that it might be best to sell that house and purchase something smaller.

She smiled at the thought. Aunt Maude would likely turn over in her grave at the very idea. The home had been in her father's family since shortly after the revolution, over a hundred years.

Well, it wasn't something she had to decide this minute. And she couldn't sit there all day staring out the window at the falling snow, either. The children would be rising soon and she needed to have something prepared for their breakfast. Just as she was contemplating exactly what to cook, Jonah scurried down the ladder from the loft.

They'd spent the better part of the day yesterday cleaning up there and hanging fresh sheets to separate the girls' side from Jonah's.

"Good morning." Ansley smiled at him and her heart thrilled at his returning lopsided grin.

"Guess I slept a little longer than usual," he said.

"I'm sure it was just all the hard work we did yesterday."

He nodded. "It was nice sleeping in my old bed, too." He frowned. "Not that I don't like Uncle Seth's house."

"I know." Any other words she might have offered fell flat before they reached her tongue. Jonah stepped to the window and glanced outside. Darkness was fading into the soft light of cloud-covered, snowy morning, revealing the beauty of the new day.

"Uncle Seth won't be coming to get us for church in this." He grinned at her. "Looks like you're stuck with us another night."

"As much as I was looking forward to service today, the thought of having you children for another night pleases me. Now, what should we have for breakfast?"

"I thought I'd go down to the cold cellar and bring up some bacon. Aunt Teddy left some eggs, too."

Ansley watched as he pulled on his boots, then his coat and hat. He looked very much like a young man, rather than a boy as he stepped outside. Quick tears sprang to Ansley's eyes as she thought about all the things Rose would miss—milestones in her children's lives.

As much as she was beginning to care for Seth and Teddy, she just couldn't imagine going back to Boston without at least attempting to take the children with her.

Before Jonah returned from the cold cellar, the girls woke and climbed down from the loft. They were still clad in their soft cotton nightgowns. They curled up next to Ansley on the sofa, snuggling close for warmth.

When Lily began to shake, Ansley drew her closer, thinking the girl was cold. Then as she pulled the little girl onto her lap, she glimpsed tears on her cheeks.

"Sweetheart," Ansley said, alarm seizing her. "Whatever is the matter?"

"I thought Ma and Pa would be here."

Next to her, Hannah pressed her head against Ansley's arm and she knew the other little girl was crying, as well.

"Girls, tell me why you thought your parents would be here."

Lily's watery gaze nearly dissolved Ansley. "We left when they left. So I thought if we came back, so would they."

Ansley prayed as she never had before. For wisdom and understanding and the right words to speak. "Is that what you thought, too, Hannah?"

Hannah shook her head. "No. They're in heaven. I just miss them more since we're at our old house."

"You little darlings. I bet your mama is looking down from heaven right now wishing she could hold you and comfort you."

"Do you really think so?" Lily asked. "Sarah Wayne says when someone goes to heaven, they're so happy playing with Jesus that they never even think about anyone down here."

Irritation wound its way through Ansley's stomach. "Well, Sarah Wayne doesn't know everything. Are you going to believe her or me?"

Lily grinned. "You, Auntie Ansley."

"Well, I should say so."

Jonah returned with an armload of meat. He set his bundle on the counter and removed his coat and boots.

"We're cold, Jonah," Hannah said.

He nodded. "Temperature's dropping. I'll get the fire built back up."

"Shouldn't I be doing that? After all, you're a child."

Hannah giggled. "Jonah builds the fire every day. That's one of his chores."

"Really?"

Jonah nodded and grinned. "We don't got servants here."

Ansley knew she was never going to live down the fact that she had servants for household tasks. Honestly, the children must think her the laziest person they ever met.

Ansley shooed the girls up the ladder to get dressed, while she set about frying bacon, which she could do quite well. Flapjacks, on the other hand, weren't her forte.

She did her best and the children ate without commenting on the burnt edges of the flapjacks. At least the bacon had turned out well.

They spent the morning and early afternoon staying warm, reading, talking and generally enjoying each other. By midafternoon, the snow had stopped falling and the windows frosted over. A beef stew bubbled on the stove to go with the a loaf of fresh bread Teddy had brought the day before.

Jonah had filled the wood box to overflowing to get

them through the day. By suppertime, they heard the jingle of bells outside. The children ran to the door. "Uncle Seth hitched up the sleigh!" Ansley's heart sank a little. She'd thought she'd have another night with the children.

"Does that mean we don't get to stay home another night?" Hannah asked.

"It looks like Uncle Seth is here to take you back home."

Seth kicked the snow from his boots before he entered the house.

"You must be freezing," Ansley murmured. "Would you like some coffee to warm you up?"

He shook his head. "It's getting colder. I'd better just collect the children and get them home." He included all three with his gaze. "Get your things and make sure to bring your quilts to cover up with."

The children moved slowly to do as they were told, clearly wishing to stay put. Though she'd never encourage disobedience, she couldn't help but be warmed by their resistance to leaving.

When they were in the loft, Ansley turned to Seth. "Are you sure they should go out in this?"

"They'll be okay." He glanced around. "You've been working hard."

Still processing the fact that he was here to take the children away, Ansley shrugged. "We cleaned upstairs yesterday. Today, we've been lazy and cozy by the fire."

He motioned toward the kitchen. "Smells good."

Gracious, the stew. How on earth would she ever eat it all? Even over several days. She'd planned for the children to eat supper with her and thought she'd serve it for lunch the following day. "Are you sure you can't all just stay for supper?"

"We'd best not. It's starting to snow again."

Bedding dropped from the loft onto the floor and the children climbed down behind it. They remained somber as Ansley helped them fold the quilts.

Seth gathered up Lily in his arms and they trudged out into the snow to the waiting sleigh. Turning to her, Seth lifted his arm in farewell. "I'll be back over to check on you tomorrow."

"Then why didn't you just wait until then to get the children?" she muttered under her breath.

As she listened to the jingling of the bells, she closed the door and glanced around. Suddenly the cabin that just minutes ago had seemed so cozy and warm felt just as large and cold as Aunt Maude's mansion.

Chapter 11

Ansley filled the evening pulling Frank's and Rose's clothing from the wardrobe and packing it in the crates Teddy and Seth had provided. The bedding had been put in a pile to be laundered as soon as the weather cleared, and Ansley had borrowed bedding from Mrs. Boatwright to tide her over until she washed these. She unpacked her own gowns from her trunks and hung them in the wardrobe, barely able to fit them all.

Guilt struck her at her overabundance. Rose may have enjoyed the benefit of nice furnishings but her wardrobe was sparse by comparison. There were only four dresses, and only one that Ansley felt proper for wearing to town. Rose would have loved the gowns Ansley had purchased for her. She had left those in her trunks. Teddy might like to have them. They would need minor alterations to fit her, but much less than would be necessary for Ansley to wear them.

As she worked in Rose's room, she hadn't realized the house was growing cold. But as soon as she stepped into the kitchen and living area, she realized she had let the fire die.

"Oh!" How could she have been so stupid? Jonah had shown her how to make the fire, but had suggested she at least try to keep feeding it so she wouldn't have to work from the ground up to build one. And now she would have to do just that.

Trying to remember the steps Jonah had taken to build the fire, she got small pieces of wood from the kindling box and set them in the bottom of the fireplace, then tried to light it. The wood absolutely refused to catch. After several frustrating failed attempts, she gave up and leaned back against the wall, catching her breath and sending a desperate plea to heaven. As she stood to go into the kitchen, where it was warmer, her gown snagged on a wood plank, and as she turned, a board dislodged and hung down.

She frowned, curiosity leading her as she reached up and pulled. The board and the one underneath gave way. Clearly Frank had built a hiding place into his walls. Not an extremely large one, but big enough to hide all the things she had brought for Rose. The gold French mantel clock and candelabras, plus all the jewels from Aunt Maude's collection.

The extra movement helped keep her warm as she went to the trunks and moved the valuables to the hiding place. Afterward she replaced the boards and stood back, satisfied to note Frank had crafted the recess well. Nothing about the boards would make anyone suspicious.

After she ate her supper, Ansley looked at the nearly full pot of stew and realized she'd have to take it to the cold cellar. If she left it outside, no telling what animals she would draw to the porch. She wrapped up in her coat and scarf and ventured out.

As snow seeped into her shoes, she realized how woefully inappropriate they were for this sort of life. She made a mental note to ask Teddy's help to purchase attire fitting for the Kansas prairie.

The cold cellar was thankfully just a few steps past the porch at the side of the house, and she reached it in no time, though the deep snow crept beneath her clothing and left her wet and miserable. She tried to open the door, but heavy snow covered it, and she couldn't make it budge. She had no idea where Rose and Frank might have kept their shovels. She was pretty sure she'd never make it the thirty feet to the barn. She had no choice but to cover the pot and hope the animals stayed away.

Inside she changed out of her wet clothes and sat down at the table. How foolish of her to think she could live alone in a cabin without others to help her.

Ansley finished washing her supper dishes just as darkness enveloped the skies and crept into the cabin. She lit the oil lamp and carried it into her room, and then set it on the table next to the bed. She went to the fireplace and took down the bed warmer. Thankfully the stove still had embers burning inside. She grabbed the small metal scoop and shoveled the embers into the warmer, then closed it tightly to keep the embers from scorching the sheets.

Back in the bedroom, she moved the warmer over the sheets before she climbed into bed. As much as she hated to use Rose's dusty bedding, she knew her own quilt wasn't going to be warm enough against the cold.

She removed her shoes, but decided to sleep in her

clothes for more warmth. The wool dress would keep her much warmer than a linen nightdress.

When she finally crawled under the covers, the bed warmer had done its job, and combined with the three quilts and her heavy clothing, she felt warm for the first time since noon. She closed her eyes and drifted to sleep.

The moon was high when she bolted upright, awakened by…something. There it was again. A scratching and groaning coming from outside the cabin door. Her thoughts went to the valuables hidden in the wall. Had someone seen her hide them? Fear caught in her throat and she realized she had no gun with which to protect herself. If she lived through this night, she would definitely speak to Mr. Dobson about procuring one. She reached under the covers and pulled the handle of the bed warmer, then slowly swung her legs around. When she stood up, she nearly squealed at the freezing cold floor under her feet.

The scratching came again as she reached the cabin door. She brandished the bed warmer like a sword.

"Who's there?" she called out. "I have a weapon." Perhaps the intruder would assume she was aiming a gun at the door. After all, who didn't have a gun in these parts? Only her.

The scratching came again, followed by a bark this time. Ansley frowned. Who brought their dog with them if they were up to no good?

She called out again, and still the only answer was a bark and then a whine. That did it. There was a dog outside her cabin trying to get in. And the varmint had probably eaten her stew. A truly pitiful, hairy creature sat in front of her door. "Why, you're the fellow that came by last week. Don't you have a home?"

He whined in answer and jumped up on the door, knocking it open and nearly knocking Ansley off her feet. She stumbled back as the massive animal, much bigger than it had appeared on her porch, pounced on her, placing its paws on her chest. "Gracious," she hollered. "Get down."

The dog obeyed instantly and sat in front of her, tongue out, tail wagging. She tilted her head and eyed the hairy mutt. He was…sort of cute, she supposed. She'd never owned, nor had a desire to own, a dog. But she wasn't without mercy.

"For goodness' sake, I can't send you back out to freeze, can I?" He gave a quick bark and started to jump on her again. Ansley stepped back and pointed. "No. Stay down."

Immediately he sat.

Smiling, she patted his wet head and closed the door. "Well, I'm sorry there's no fire in the fireplace. I'm afraid I'm incompetent in that department. I bet you'd love to lie in front of a fire to dry off. But maybe I can dry you off a different way." She went into the bedroom and grabbed her oldest nightgown from her trunk. She stoked up the kitchen stove and went to work trying to get the beast more comfortable. An hour later, between the fire in the stove and her vigorous rubbing, he was dry. She fed him the rest of the bread and set the pail of water on the floor. Then she filled the bed warmer again and headed to the bedroom. The dog trotted after her, happily wagging his tail.

"Now, listen. You may sleep on the floor anywhere in this cabin. But do not jump on my sister's sofa and do not under any circumstances sleep in my bed. Is that understood?"

Ansley had always believed animals to be much more

intelligent than humans gave them credit for. So she hoped he had understood. She pointed to the throw rug next to her bed and said, "Down," since that had seemed to work earlier. He dropped to his belly and rested his head between his paws. With a sigh, he closed his eyes. Satisfied, Ansley crawled back into bed and hoped for a few more hours of uninterrupted sleep.

The sun peeked through her window, waking her early the next morning. She snuggled into the cozy warmth of her bed, hating to push aside the covers and expose herself to the freezing cold cabin. Then she realized the bed might have been a little warmer than it should have, even with three quilts. She opened her eyes and ventured a glance, then let out a heavy sigh. Clearly the dog hadn't understood after all. Curled up next to her, he was sleeping peacefully.

Well, she had prayed she wouldn't freeze to death. Perhaps this dog was simply an answer to her prayer and a promise from the Lord that He would indeed take care of her throughout the winter.

Seth frowned as he approached the cabin where he'd left Ansley the day before. The children had been sullen until they began talking about their visit with Ansley. Then they chattered incessantly. Aunt Ansley said this, Aunt Ansley let us do that. We should have stayed for supper since Aunt Ansley went to all that trouble to cook for us.

Seth knew he had behaved rashly when he made the sudden decision to hitch the sleigh and go pick them up. Jonah had worried himself sick about whether she could keep the fire going. This morning, he wouldn't stop pestering Seth until he made good on his promise to come over to the cabin and check on her.

And it appeared the boy had been right. There wasn't a hint of smoke coming from the chimney or the stovepipe above the kitchen stove. His stomach clenched with worry. He remembered how ignorant Rose had been about everything when she first arrived in Kansas as Frank's new bride.

He inwardly kicked himself. He should have made certain Ansley could take care of herself before rushing the children out of the cabin yesterday. Teddy had grown up building fires, cooking. Could Ansley even boil a pot of coffee? Well, yes, he knew she could do that much. And the stew had smelled edible. But she had to have a fire to make coffee or cook.

He pulled on the reins and the sleigh came to a halt in front of the cabin. Everything looked cold and dark inside, and as he stepped onto the porch, he worried that he might find Ansley half-frozen. He frowned at the pot of stew on the porch, upended but without a drop of food. An animal likely got to it. He'd have to tell her to use the cold storage unless she wanted to draw wolves or bobcats.

He picked up the pot and knocked on the door. A bark greeted him from the other side of the door. What on earth? He knocked again and again heard the bark, followed by a thud—presumably a dog was jumping against the door.

A knot formed in his throat. Had someone tried to take shelter in the cabin and found Ansley there? Fear and guilt combined inside of him. If something had happened to Ansley, he'd never forgive himself for his behavior toward her. Removing his pistol from his belt, he reached for the latch. He was about to shove his way in when the door opened. Ansley stood wrapped in a quilt, and a large hairy dog stood in front of her. The mutt gave a low warning growl. Obviously, he had the same idea that Seth had—he wanted to protect Ansley.

"It's okay," Ansley said softly, scratching the dog's head. Instantly, the animal trotted away and flopped down next to the kitchen table. Ansley looked up and gave Seth a rueful grin. "He scratched at my door overnight. I think he likes me."

"That's the mutt I threw out of here last week, isn't it?"

She nodded, grinning and motioned to the pot he still held. "He smelled the stew. At least it didn't go to waste."

Seth set the pot on the counter by the washbowl. "I'll put the word out in case someone is missing him."

Her brow creased for an instant, and then she nodded. "I suppose we should do that. I doubt his owners would want to lose him."

Seth couldn't help but smile. "You planned on keeping him?"

She shrugged. "I hadn't really thought that far ahead. But I suppose if no one claims him, he can stay."

As he had suspected, there was no fire in either the fireplace or the cookstove. "Have you been without heat since we left yesterday?"

Ansley shook her head. "I can build a fire in the kitchen stove. I'm ashamed to say, the dog and I had just climbed out of bed when you knocked. I was too cold to move and he was keeping me warm."

A chuckle from Seth's mouth made a puff of steam inside the cold cabin. "You let him sleep in your bed? You'll likely be full of fleas."

"Fleas!"

"Well, dogs have fleas. And that dog has enough hair to hide an entire town of the little critters. If you're going to keep him inside, you'll need to scrub him down with lye soap. You have some on the shelf over there."

"Oh. Well, I suppose I'd best do that today, then." She frowned, pushing out her lips as though trying to decide just how to go about accomplishing such a task.

Seth shook his head. "Let me get a good fire going in the fireplace while you light the stove, and we'll get him taken care of before I leave. But don't expect him to like it."

Relief passed across her face. "I'd appreciate it."

By the time the fire was roaring, Ansley had lit the stove and had a pot of coffee boiling. He frowned. "Aren't you going to have breakfast?"

Her face turned red. "Oh, are you hungry?"

"No. I had mine at home. But I don't see any fixings for yours." Again, he kicked himself. "I guess the snow covered over the door to the cellar?"

She nodded and quickly looked away, but not before Seth saw tears in her lovely blue-green eyes.

"Look, Ansley," he said. "I'm sorry we left you here like this. We had no idea you couldn't take care of yourself."

Her head jerked up and her eyes flashed. "I can so take care of myself. I just didn't know it was going to snow like this. I'd have gotten my supplies indoors sooner if I'd known."

"What about the fire?"

Gathering a breath, she raised her arms and let them fall against her sides. "Well, yes, the fire is a problem. I suppose I should have watched how you made that one."

Taken off guard by her sudden humility, Seth reached out and gripped her shoulder. The dog growled.

A smile tipped Ansley's lips. "Maybe with him around, I won't need a gun after all."

The dog slunk to Seth's feet, eyeing him like a bobcat would a weasel. Seth dropped his hand from Ansley's shoulder and frowned. "You don't have a gun?"

"Why, no. I've really never cared for them."

"Well, out here, people carry guns. Especially women living alone. What if someone came to your door with ill intentions? How would you protect yourself?"

Her shoulders rose and fell in an infuriating shrug that proved she had no idea of the dangers of living out here. He wished he'd fought harder to keep her from moving into the cabin.

"I suppose the dog will protect me. After all, he got your hand off my shoulder just now, didn't he?"

There was no arguing with a woman who always thought she was right.

With a growl, Seth decided to change the subject. "What do you want from the cold cellar?"

"Oh, if you tell me where to find a shovel, I can attend to that."

"Look, I'm here. I have nothing else to do, and I'm willing to help. Don't be so stubborn."

"Fine, Mr. Dobson. And for the record, I don't know what's in the cold cellar, so how would I know what I want?"

"Never mind. I'll bring up a few supplies you might need for the next couple of days. If you pack snow in the laundry tub, you should be able to keep the food good for that long."

Glad to be outside, away from the lure of Ansley's eyes and her frustrating stubbornness, he went to the barn, grabbed the shovel and cleared off the cellar door. Minutes later, he stepped around to the front to find Ansley filling the washtub with the snow as he'd suggested. He dumped the food he'd gathered: a bit of bacon, enough for breakfast for a couple of days, a deer roast and a couple of the jars—applesauce and peas—Teddy had spent the month of September putting up.

Once inside, Ansley pulled two cups from the cabinet above the stove. "Come and warm up." She poured coffee for each of them as he set the tub on the counter.

He sat at the table and picked up the spoon next to his cup. She remembered he liked sugar. Somehow, the thought that they had something in common made him feel generous. "The children were disappointed they had to go home last night. They talked about you all the way home and all through supper."

When her face brightened, he felt his chest swell. He remembered Frank saying one time that he lived a happy life with Rose, but the happiest moments were those in which something he did just for her caused her eyes to light and her mouth to smile. He wasn't sure why he had thought of that, but perhaps this was close to the feeling Frank had described.

"I don't suppose they had school today?" she asked.

Seth shook his head. "I imagine those who live in town went, but the teacher knows not to expect those who live on farms to come to school when the snow is this high."

"Not even with the sleigh?" She nodded toward the door. "It's lovely, by the way. I've always loved riding in a horse-drawn sleigh."

"So did Rose. There's a cutter in the barn that Frank and I made the first winter they were married. By the time we got it finished, they couldn't use it until the next year, though."

"Was there nothing he wouldn't do to make my sister happy?" Ansley asked, her eyes glistening. Standing, she walked over to the mantel and pulled off a familiar wooden box. "I've been admiring this since I arrived. Look at the beautiful roses carved into the cover. It's as beautifully finished as anything I've seen in Boston." With a sigh, she set the box on the table and sat back down in her chair. "Rose must have been the most blessed woman in the world to have a man who loved her so much. I just wish..."

Without thought, Seth reached over and covered her hand with his. "I'm sure she knew you loved her and didn't wish her ill for leaving you."

"That's just it. I did at times resent that she had gone off and left me all alone with Aunt Maude. And then when I never received any letters, I thought she'd forgotten all about me. I never wished her anything but happiness, but as I said, there were times I deeply resented being left alone to care for our aunt."

Seth moved his hand from hers and took hold of his cup. "Don't worry yourself about that, Ansley. It's only natural to resent it when someone leaves you to shoulder responsibilities that shouldn't be yours alone to bear."

A frown creased her brow and before she even spoke, Seth knew what she was going to say. "Do you mean like Frank and Rose leaving their children for you to raise?"

"If I said 'yes,' would you try to use it against me?" He searched her face but could find no judgment, no ulterior motive. Perhaps he didn't know her well enough to ponder what was going on inside her head, but if he had to guess, he'd say she was interested for his sake, not for her own.

When she smiled, he knew he was right. "Mr. Dobson...Seth...I appreciate your honesty."

"To be honest, I was thinking more of Teddy. She's

far too young to be taking on the responsibility of the children. Grandpa would like her to come live with him in Martin's Creek and she was all set to do so, and then the accident happened. Now that the children are settled, she could go, but she doesn't think I can raise them properly without her."

"Can you?" Ansley ducked her head as soon as she spoke. "I'm sorry, Seth. I shouldn't have asked that. Of course you can take care of them."

She'd apologized so fast, Seth didn't even have the chance to be offended by her question. "I can take care of all their physical needs. That's for sure. But I can't give them what a woman can."

Reaching over, Ansley placed a warm, slender hand on his forearm. "Those children know they are loved. That's the most important thing. A woman raised Rose and me, and take it from someone who knows, just because she was a woman didn't make her loving or compassionate."

A surge of gratitude moved through Seth. He covered her hand with his. His stomach jumped and she slipped her hand out from under his, as though she felt the same...whatever it was that had just happened between them.

Not knowing what else to say, he raised his cup to his lips and drank the now lukewarm coffee. They sat that way, silent except for the light snoring of the dog in front of the fireplace and the occasional crackling of wood. His mind drifted to Frank and Rose. Did they have mornings like this in their cozy little cabin? What would it be like to have this every day?

Chapter 12

The next week brought nothing but mud as the snow melted into the ground and turned the earth into sludge. Grateful for the supplies left by Teddy and Seth, Ansley spent the lonely days getting the cabin in order. By the time she thought she might go mad if forced to spend one more day inside the cabin, the ground was hard enough to saddle her horse and ride into town.

By midweek, there had been no one to claim the stray dog, so she'd named him Harry. Now he trotted along beside her as she made the five-mile trip into town for church.

The sun shone in abundance despite the chill in the air, which called for a coat instead of her usual shawl. Riding Bella, Ansley overtook the wagon carrying Seth, Teddy and the children within a mile of town. The girls were dressed in lovely pink dresses peeking out beneath their coats and had ribbons tied at the ends of their braids. Each beamed when Ansley commented on how pretty they looked. She turned to Jonah. "And you, fine sir, will be the envy of every man present."

His ears grew red under her praise. "Preacher says envy's a sin."

Ansley laughed. "Well, that's true."

"Will you sit on the bench with us, Aunt Ansley?" Hannah asked. "We have one with Grandpa's name on it."

Ansley's eyebrows rose at this news. In the fine churches of Boston numerous items within the sacred sanctuaries held plaques with the names of generous families, but she'd never expected it of a small-town church.

Teddy grinned up at her, apparently noting her surprise. "It's really not that much of a privilege. Mr. Carson also has his own pew, and I've never actually seen him step foot inside the church."

"Luke sits all by hisself," Lily piped up.

"Yes, because he stinks and no one wants to sit next to him."

"Hannah!" Teddy admonished. But after Ansley's hideous ride from Martin's Creek next to the man, she could imagine the child was right.

They arrived at church well before the bell rang to announce the beginning of the service. Seth parked the wagon in the yard. Ansley headed toward the post in front of the church, where several horses were tethered. As she pulled on the reins, she noticed Mr. Lane striding toward her. "May I assist you down from there, Miss Potter?"

"Certainly, thank you."

She slid into his arms. He held on just a little longer than was necessary and heat flooded Ansley's cheeks.

She was pretty sure this wasn't gentlemanly behavior, even on the prairie. Her gaze immediately fell on Seth's and she stepped from Mr. Lane's arms. Seth stood, holding Lily. His scowl told her he didn't like what he saw. Ansley's heart sped up and again she wondered why he wanted her to stay away from Mr. Lane.

"May I escort you inside, Miss Potter?" Mr. Lane asked, holding out his arm.

As she took his arm, Seth looked away and walked into the church.

"How has your first week in the cabin been?" Mr. Lane asked. "I worried about you during our little snowstorm last week."

"And yet you did not come and check to see how I was?" Ansley couldn't help but compare Mr. Lane with Seth, who had come over several times to help her. He'd applauded when she finally built a sustainable fire in the fireplace.

"I didn't want to intrude. But now that I know you are agreeable to my visits, I will make it a point to check on your welfare several times each week." He ducked his head and spoke for her ears only. "Some folks might call that courting."

"Why, Mr. Lane, I certainly said nothing about courting."

"Well, don't make up your mind just yet. Perhaps you might consider giving me a thought from time to time?"

He seemed so sincere, and he truly was a handsome gentleman. Still, she would be returning to Boston in a few weeks. So there was no point in allowing any man to call, unless it was Seth. She shoved that notion away and focused on the handsome man she was speaking with. "Mr. Lane…"

"Please, call me Mitch."

"Mr. Lane," she said again, this time more firmly. "The fact is I am returning home right after the New Year. So there is little point in pursuing anything more than friendship."

"Well, Miss Potter," he said with a wry grin. "Let's be friends." He winked and left her standing next to the Dobsons' pew.

How outrageous for him to wink at her and walk away. She felt a tug on her sleeve and glanced down to find Teddy looking amused as she scooted over to allow Ansley to sit. "It appears you've caught the eye of a very fine-looking man."

"I'm sure I don't know what you mean," she replied, slipping into the seat beside Teddy.

"You certainly do know what I mean," Teddy whispered. "And unless I miss my guess, Seth is stewing in his own juices because that man escorted you in. You may just have not one, but two admirers."

"For goodness' sake."

Thankfully, service began just then, preventing further conversation on the subject.

Until dinner, that is. Teddy had outdone herself, piling the table with roasted chicken, potatoes, cabbage cooked with pork fat and biscuits so fluffy they'd put the best chef in Boston to shame.

"Now," Teddy said as soon as Seth finished the blessing. "Whatever was Mr. Lane saying to you that caused you to blush?"

Ansley glanced around the table and everyone except Seth stared at her, waiting for an answer. Seth had begun filling his plate in surly silence.

"It was nothing, really. He—wanted to come calling, that's all."

This brought Seth's head up. "It's not proper for a man to call on a woman who lives alone."

Ansley was just about to remind him he had spent several hours alone with her in the cabin a number of times. Teddy waved away his comment and spoke before Ansley could. "Oh, there are ways around that. For instance, on the nights he comes to call, I can be at the cabin to chaperone." She angled a sideways glance at Ansley. "But don't worry, I can make myself scarce."

"Aunt Ansley wants to court that man in the black suit?" Jonah asked. His face was a mirror of Seth's, scowl and all.

Hannah handed her plate to Seth, who began filling it carefully. "Sarah Wayne says a woman your age ain't very likely to catch a man," she said.

"Hannah! Hold your tongue," Teddy admonished. "I declare, you children need to learn better manners. But then, I suppose it's my fault for bringing it up in the first place." She sent Ansley a look of apology.

But suddenly, Ansley saw the humor of it all. Was this what it would be like having curious, insightful children at every meal?

"It's all right, Teddy." She turned her attention to Hannah. "What else does Sarah Wayne have to say about my prospects of catching a husband?"

"She said you'd best set your cap for Uncle Seth, because you both love us and you probably never would catch another fella. And from the looks of things, Uncle Seth ain't likely to go looking for a wife anyway. So you might as well take him."

Seth cleared his throat. "Hannah, fill your mouth with food and stop talking."

"But Auntie Ansley asked me what Sarah Wayne said."

"Well, you've told her, so get to your dinner and hush."

Teddy sent a sly look toward Seth, and then toward Ansley. Ansley shook her head at the young woman she had begun to see as a younger sister. With a laugh, Teddy filled her mouth with food as Seth had instructed Hannah to do.

"Hannah," Ansley said. "You may tell your friend Sarah Wayne that I am not setting my cap for any man in Kansas. I am returning to Boston after Christmas and there are a dozen men waiting to court me." Which wasn't far from the truth. Of course, they were just after her money rather than her heart. But they wanted to court her nonetheless.

Her words, though intended to be facetious, caused an instant uproar from the children. Jonah's brown eyes looked at her from beneath long dark lashes. "You mean you're not going to live here? I thought that's why you moved into the cabin."

"No, Jonah," she said. "I moved in to feel close to your mama while I'm in Prairie Chicken."

Lily's wail took her attention away from the boy. "But if you go, we'll never see you again. Please don't go back to Boston, Auntie Ansley. We love you. We need you." Instantly, the child worked herself into tears.

Caught up in a conversation she wasn't ready for, Ansley sought out Teddy's support. The young woman slipped her arm around Lily's shoulders. "Honey, of course we'll see Aunt Ansley. Now that she knows about you, she'll come back for visits and maybe we can go to Boston to visit her from time to time."

Ansley couldn't help but wonder if Teddy truly meant that. She hadn't given up hope of having the children with her in Boston, if nothing more than for long visits. After all, when they were older and ready to further their education, they might want to come live with her and attend college. But those were thoughts she knew instinctively she'd best keep to herself.

Seth cleared his throat, and when Ansley looked his way, she noted his eyes piercing into her, as though he knew the direction of her thoughts. Her heart sank. It appeared one unguarded moment had destroyed all the progress they had made toward an amicable existence.

Bone-weary but incredibly satisfied with the results of the hunting trip he and Jonah had taken, Seth set the brake on the wagon, grateful to be home. Teddy met them at the door and caught Jonah up in a tight hug. Then she scrunched her nose. "You two need baths."

Jonah grinned. "Yep. We got ourselves good and dirty, like real men."

Rolling her eyes, she took his coat and glanced at Seth. "Wonder where he heard that."

Chuckling, Seth slipped out of his own coat and hung it on the peg. "What did you expect us to do? Bathe in the freezing cold river?"

"That's what a real man would have done." Teddy scruffed Jonah's hair. "Go fill up the heavy pot with water and hang it on the hook over the fireplace. We'll have you cleaned up in no time." She turned to Seth. "I'll have some coffee on in a jiffy, but supper is still a couple of hours away."

"Where are the girls?" Normally, after a trip, the girls met him with squeals and hugs and kisses. He missed that.

"Ansley borrowed the wagon after school and took them to Mrs. Boatwright's to play with the Anderson children. They're staying in town for dinner."

Alarm and annoyance seized him simultaneously. “Ansley is driving the wagon home with the girls—in the dark?”

Teddy’s lips twitched as she placed the coffeepot on the stove. “Are you worried about Ansley or the girls?”

He frowned. “What’s that supposed to mean?”

Her shrug was maddening, as though she knew a secret. “You know what it means. I think you are beginning to care about our Ansley.”

“Of course I care about her. She’s the children’s aunt.”

“And what is she to you, Seth Dobson?”

“Other than a source of constant irritation? Not much.” But even as he said the words, he knew they weren’t exactly true. And from the look on her face, so did Teddy. To her credit, she clamped her lips together and didn’t argue.

“Did you bring back the patterns I asked for?”

Seth had taken advantage of the hunting trip to stop by Martin’s Creek to check on their grandfather. While there he’d stopped at the mercantile, which carried more items than the general store in Prairie Chicken.

“Yes, the dress patterns, and the dolls for the girls’ Christmas. I had to sneak out to pick up the new rifle for Jonah.”

He’d also picked up a book of poetry for Teddy and the book, *Jane Eyre,* she’d been wanting.

“Good. The dress patterns are for Ansley. She is going to make over some of the dresses she bought for Rose and give them to Hannah and Lily for Christmas. Speaking of Ansley, did you get what I asked you to pick up for her?”

Seth nodded. “*Wuthering Heights*. Personally, I don’t see why you don’t just let her borrow yours.”

"Because there's nothing like opening up a new book that belongs to you. Besides, we can't very well have her over for Christmas and not have a gift for her, can we?"

Thankfully, the coffee started to boil before she could expect an answer. The fact was Seth had made a few purchases of his own for his family's Christmas. And he'd included something for Ansley. But he hadn't decided whether to give her his gift. He'd just have to wait and see.

"What time is Ansley due back here with the girls?" he asked. "Does she even know how to handle a team of horses? George over at the livery said she was going to rent a wagon that first day she came and she couldn't keep the horses pulling together."

"I've been teaching her, and she's a quick learner, so I'm confident she'll do fine."

She poured him a cup of coffee. "Honestly, Seth, if it worries you, ride into town and escort her home. But I'd take a bath first. You smell suspiciously like Luke Carson."

Chapter 13

Ansley dropped her nieces off to play with the Anderson children and then headed to the general store, hoping to purchase Christmas gifts for Jonah. She had decided to give Teddy two of Rose's new gowns for Christmas. She couldn't decide whether to buy a gift for Seth. Surely that would seem too forward.

She had been alone with her thoughts so much at the cabin that she'd had time to consider some things. The children loved her, but they needed Seth and they needed to be close to their parents' memories. After she finished at the general store, she would venture to the telegraph office and call off the custody case. She would miss the children when she returned to Boston, but she had the means to come and visit often and she would have even more means after the sale of Aunt Maude's mansion.

Seeing movement on the floor near the back of the

store, she peeked around the table filled with baking powder and bags of flour and cornmeal and spied a little girl on the floor with a book in her hands. This could only be the infamous Sarah Wayne. The girl had red braids and even from the side, Ansley could see her face was covered in freckles. She couldn't be more than ten years old.

"Sarah, let's go," the woman at the counter called.

Ansley could barely contain her laughter as the little girl tossed the book toward the table. It slid to the floor, but she didn't seem to notice. The child stopped dead as she spotted Ansley. Her mouth dropped open and her eyes filled with dread. Her red eyebrows lifted in a silent plea as she placed a finger over her mouth, begging Ansley not to reveal her secret.

"Sarah! Now, young lady."

"Coming, Ma."

The little girl brushed past and scurried out the door. Curious, Ansley walked to the table and picked up the book from the floor. She turned it over in her hand, glanced up to make sure no one was watching and slowly opened the cover. Ten minutes later, she was still standing there, reading a fascinating tale of a white mountain man with an Indian wife. She couldn't put it down.

"Reading something interesting, Miss Potter?"

Ansley jumped and dropped the novel. "Mr. Lane! Gracious, you gave me a fright."

"Ah, that was not my intention. Here, allow me." He bent and picked up the book from the floor. Glancing at the cover, he pursed his lips with obvious amusement.

"Give me that." Ansley jerked the book from his hands. "Honestly. A little girl dropped it and I picked it up. I certainly wasn't…" She was going to say, "reading it." But one look at the handsome face and twinkling eyes of the man towering over her and she gave up even trying to fib. Laughter burst from her lips. "You caught me, Mr. Lane. I'd decided to peek inside the cover and suddenly I couldn't put the book down."

He joined in her laughter and took the book from her hands. "Allow me to purchase this for you so you can finish the enthralling tale."

"Gracious, no!" She could only imagine what Aunt Maude would have said about her reading such drivel.

But Mr. Lane was not to be deterred. "Nonsense. There's no shame in it."

"Well, go ahead then. I'm as bad as Sarah Wayne."

"Who?"

Shaking her head, Ansley waved away his question. "She's a little girl in my nieces' and nephew's school who reads these things and regales her fellow students with all kinds of stories and sage advice on courting. It's silly, but it makes me laugh."

"Then I have Miss Wayne to thank for the pleasure of hearing that laughter, don't I?"

Ansley's cheeks warmed as they seemed to do every time this man approached her.

He paid for the book and handed it to her. "Now you have shared your secret love of dime novels with me, I have a confession to make, as well."

Secret love of dime novels! Of all the…

"Well, you know quite well I confessed no such thing, and perhaps I am not interested in your confession."

"Please, Miss Potter. Indulge me."

The man was impossible. And somehow she always felt as though he was mocking her, which was disconcerting to say the least. "Well, fine. Do go on."

He opened the door of the general store and they stepped outside to a cloudy sky that promised another snow. "My secret is I saw you through the window and couldn't help but come inside and say hello."

Ansley gasped. He had seen her through the window? Reading a dime novel? How many other townsfolk had walked by and seen her doing the same?

Humiliated, all she wanted was to climb on her horse and ride to her cabin. "Well, you've said hello. And I thank you for the book, but I must be going."

His eyes clouded over, becoming as gray as the sky. "I had hoped to persuade you to join me for an early supper at Mrs. Boatwright's."

The truth of the matter was that she and the girls would be eating supper at Mrs. Boatwright's anyway. And what was wrong with a young lady enjoying a nice supper with a polite, handsome gentleman? "Since my nieces and I were already planning supper at Mrs. Boatwright's, you may join us, Mr. Lane."

His eyebrows rose and a wide smile lit up his face. "I'm delighted."

"And surprised, I'd venture to say."

He chuckled. "A little. So far you haven't seemed too receptive to my attentions."

"Mr. Lane. I'm happy to have you join us for supper, but please do not mistake my invitation for anything other than a token of friendship. As I've said before, I will be leaving Kansas right after Christmas."

Mr. Lane patted the hand tucked in the bend of his elbow. "Then I will enjoy the company of a lovely, gracious young woman as often as she'll allow until she goes back to Boston." He smiled at her. "If, that is, she has no objection."

Well, he'd certainly accepted her rebuff quickly enough. "I've no objection whatsoever."

The boardinghouse was in an uproar when they arrived.

"Oh, I'm so glad you're here," Mrs. Boatwright said, ushering her toward the stairs.

Fear seized Ansley. "Are the girls all right?"

"What?" Mrs. Boatwright gave a wave. "Yes, yes. They're playing in the library with the Anderson children."

"Then what…?"

"Alice is having her baby."

Ansley gasped. "But I just spoke with her an hour ago and she gave no indication."

"Well, she's not a new mother. And fourth babies come so quickly."

"Oh, goodness. Is the doctor with her?"

Mrs. Boatwright frowned. "The closest doctor is in Martin's Creek and there was no time to go after him just for a baby. But Franny Blake is with her. She's delivered just about every baby in this town over the past twenty years. As a matter of fact, she delivered your own sister's children. Now, go. Franny could use an extra pair of hands, and I have customers to attend."

"But Mrs. Boatwright, I am here with my nieces."

"So? They're fine. Besides, it's good the Anderson children have other children to occupy them at a time like this."

"But I have never been present during childbirth. I couldn't possibly…"

Mr. Lane cleared his throat. "Excuse me. We've come for an early supper." He sounded annoyed.

Mrs. Boatwright and Ansley turned. "Oh! Mr. Lane. I'm so sorry. I'm afraid our supper will have to wait for another day." She sighed and set her chin. "My friend needs me, I'm afraid."

He released a breath and nodded. "I'll hold you to that."

Mrs. Boatwright scowled. "Yes, yes. There's no time for this." She waved toward the restaurant. "Feel free to go eat your supper alone, Mr. Lane." Then she shoved Ansley up the steps. "Go!"

Ansley gathered her skirt and hurried up the stairs. She paused for an instant outside of Alice's room, but a cry from within sent her scurrying inside. The woman was writhing in pain, and as she turned and saw Ansley she reached for her. Ansley rushed forward and took her hand. "It's all right. Squeeze all you need to."

When the contraction ended, Alice gathered a breath and sank back onto her pillow, spent.

"Oh, Ansley. I wish Peter were here. This is the first baby I've had without him just outside my door."

"Shh." Ansley dipped a cloth in the basin of water on the table next to the bed. She wrung it out and wiped it gently over Alice's forehead. "As soon as the baby arrives, I'll send him a telegram."

"Thank you." Her face twisted in pain as another contraction seized her.

"Won't be long now," the midwife announced. "Give us a good push."

Alice bore down until Franny instructed her to stop. Then she sank back again, breathless.

In minutes, a pretty baby girl came into the world with lusty cries, a little pink body and a tuft of silky red hair.

The midwife loosely wrapped the baby and handed her to Ansley.

Stupefied, Ansley took the baby, but she couldn't move. "What do I do?"

The midwife rolled her eyes. "Clean her up and give her to her mother, obviously."

"Let me get a peek at her first," Alice said.

Ansley carried the baby to Alice's bedside so she could peek at her new daughter.

Alice gave a weary smile and tears misted her eyes. "She looks like Fiona."

"I'll have her back to you in no time."

"Thank you." She closed her eyes and drifted to sleep while the midwife finished her ministrations and Ansley bathed the baby.

An hour later, Ansley gathered up the soiled sheets and left Alice cooing to her new little girl.

She carried the sheets downstairs and tossed them inside the closet where Viola collected all the soiled sheets for washday. She went to the dining room to share the good news with the children.

To her surprise, Mr. Lane was still sitting in the dining room, finishing a meal. He sat with the Anderson children and her nieces, who had also eaten. Had he stayed so long just to see her again? The very idea seemed ludicrous and caused her cheeks to flush.

The little group looked up as Ansley approached. She smiled at Fiona. "You have a new little sister."

Charley moaned. "A girl?"

"I told you it would be a girl." Fiona's smug grin brought a laugh to Ansley's lips.

"May we see Mama?" Fiona asked.

Ansley touched the girl's shoulder. "She and the baby are resting right now. But you can see her later."

Mr. Lane stood and pulled out the only empty chair at the table. "May I order you something to eat?"

"That's kind, but I truly couldn't eat a thing."

Mitch Lane didn't sit down and join her. Instead he

pulled some coins from his pocket and set them on the table, presumably for his own meal. "I'm afraid I must be going. I will be seeing you again soon, Miss Potter."

Ansley watched him walk away. When he reached the doorway between the restaurant and boardinghouse, an idea hit her. She rose quickly and caught up to him just as he was about to leave through the front door. "Mr. Lane. Please wait."

He turned. "Is something wrong?"

She shook her head. "No. Everything is fine. But I wonder if I may impose on you for one favor?"

His face brightened and the corners of his lips moved upward into a smile. "It would be my pleasure."

"Will you get a message to Teddy Dobson for me?"

His eyes narrowed and the smile left his face. "Teddy?"

"Seth's sister. Seth's been out of town, but if you see him first, you can certainly give the message to him." Ansley knew full well the two men didn't care for each other. Still she had little choice but to send word with Mr. Lane. "I'm supposed to be bringing the girls back to the Dobsons' place after supper, but as you can see, Alice needs me to stay and help care for her older children. If you can ask Teddy or Seth to come and get the girls I'd be grateful."

She drew in her lower lip between her teeth. "I suppose I can ask them to take care of Harry myself when he comes to get the girls."

"Harry?"

"He's a dog that came to me during the snowstorm. I haven't found his owners yet, so I'm beginning to think he's mine. He's quite protective, which gives me comfort when I'm alone at night."

"I see. You're the type of woman who takes in strays."

He offered a wry grin. "Would you believe me if I told you I'm a stray?"

"Mr. Lane…"

He held up his hand. "I'm sorry. That was too forward of me."

"Yes, it was," Ansley said firmly. But inwardly she was beginning to soften toward this man. Of course she'd be gone in a few weeks, but then, a lot could happen in a short time when the right person came along. She wondered if Sarah Wayne would agree, and she had to force herself not to smile.

He took hold of her hand and pressed his lips to her knuckles. "Rest assured, I will deliver your message."

Thanking him, Ansley closed the door behind him and returned to the dining room. She found Mrs. Boatwright talking to the children. She turned to Ansley. "She's a beautiful little girl. First baby we've ever had born under this roof. I feel almost like a grandmother." She winked at the children.

Ansley couldn't help but smile at the elderly woman. So much for not allowing children in her boardinghouse. It seemed the Andersons had rolled into town and turned this woman's world upside down. Still, she wasn't young, and running after a two-year-old like Willie was out of the question.

"I'm making arrangements to stay for a few days to help Alice with the children."

Relief washed over Mrs. Boatwright's lined face. "I'm sure Alice would appreciate it." She stood. "I'll go get your room ready and bring the children's bedding from Alice's room."

Ansley watched her go, glad she was available to help, but at the same time, aware she only had a few more weeks with her own nieces and nephew. She wanted to make every second count. But now wasn't the time for selfishness. Alice needed her. And she knew if Rose had been in this situation, she would have wanted someone there to offer assistance. Relaxing, she resigned herself to giving of herself the next few days. She turned to Alice's children. "Finish up your supper, and I will take you to see your ma and the baby."

Chapter 14

Seth stabbed at the hay in the trough and pitched it into the horse stall. Sweat trickled down his face and all he could think about was Mitch Lane's smirk the day before when he'd passed along Ansley's message. Teddy had driven the wagon over to the cabin this morning to gather up some clothing for Ansley, but so far she hadn't returned.

The night before, Seth had retrieved Harry. The big, furry animal had been following him around ever since. Even now, he was sitting in the corner, watching every move Seth made.

Was Seth the only person who could see through Mitch's facade? Ansley probably believed the lying thief was sincere in his attentions toward her. But Seth knew better. Not that Ansley wasn't pretty and smart and kind—all the things a man looked for in a wife. But despite those attributes, one thing was certain…

Mitch Lane was after her wealth. Seth knew firsthand the man wasn't above stealing, but apparently he had decided to try to steal her heart rather than simply her possessions. But how did he tell a proud woman like Ansley that she was being taken for a fool?

Seth turned to Harry. "How are we going to convince her, boy?"

Harry stood, tail wagging. Seth felt silly confiding in a dog, but who else could he share his concern with? Teddy would make more of it than it was. She had already hinted there was romance in the air between Ansley and Seth. Which was ridiculous. Teddy would see his worry about Mitch as nothing more than jealousy.

He hung the pitchfork between two nails he'd pounded into the wall and scuffed Harry's head. Harry followed him out of the barn as the wagon came rattling into the yard.

Teddy had barely pulled the wagon to a stop before she jumped down. Seth's heart sped up when he saw the worry on her face. He hurried across the yard and met her. "What happened?"

"Someone..." She gulped in a breath, leaving Seth to imagine the worst.

"Tell me what happened. Did someone hurt you?"

She shook her head, placing her hands flat on his chest as he gripped her arms. "It's the cabin. Someone has ransacked it."

"What do you mean?" His mind conjured up the image of Mitch Lane rummaging through Ansley's trunks that day on the road.

"The cabin. Someone was in there. Do you think they were trying to steal from Ansley?"

"I'd say that's a safe bet."

"Then we have to go to the sheriff!"

"We will, but I want to go see the cabin first."

Seth saddled Brewster and rode the three miles to the cabin with Harry trotting along after him. He opened the door and was instantly filled with anger. Ansley's things had been tossed around the rooms. Clothes and shoes and books were strewn from one end to the other. Even pots and pans and dishes were lying on the floor, some broken. The wooden box Ansley had admired had been tossed aside and lay open. Seth knew exactly who had done this.

He mounted Brewster, planning to ride into town, inform Ansley of the intruder and escort her to the sheriff's office. But still seething at Mitch Lane's audacity, he turned Brewster toward Carson's house instead. Harry followed along after him as he made his way onto Carson's property and to his door.

Luke Carson greeted him. The simple man grinned and offered his hand after Seth dismounted. "Good to see you, Seth. Everything okay?"

"I came to see Mitch Lane. You seen him around?"

A frown creased Luke's brow. "Not since yesterday. Pa's up in arms about it. Said Mitch didn't show up today, and he had a job for him over at the Rainers'."

Seth could imagine what sort of job. It was common knowledge that with Seth's property out of the question, Mr. Carson had turned his attention to the property on the other side of his. The Rainers had fallen on hard times, and Carson clearly planned to take full advantage of their bad luck.

If Mitch had hightailed it out of the area, he must've gotten his hands on whatever he'd been looking for at Ansley's. The thought sent waves of anger through Seth. "Any idea if he's gone, or maybe sick?"

Luke shook his head. "I went and checked his room.

Seems all his things are missing. There ain't no sign he was ever here." Luke shielded his eyes from the bright sun. "You got business with Mitch?"

"No. Just wanted to ask him a couple of questions."

"Well, if you find him, tell him Pa's looking for him."

Seth promised to do so and climbed into Brewster's saddle. Snow was beginning to fall by the time he reached town. Large, wet flakes covered his hat and Brewster's mane.

When he walked into the boardinghouse, he saw Ansley coming down the stairs, holding on to little Willie's chubby hand as she kept his toddler legs stable. She smiled when she saw Seth and his heart picked up. As much as he'd love to make this a social call, he had to tell Ansley she had been the victim of a robbery, and he had an idea who might be to blame.

Ansley stared in horror at the sight that greeted her when she walked into the cabin behind the sheriff and Seth Dobson. Her trunks were broken up and strung around the room.

"Who on earth would have done such a thing?" She angled her gaze at Seth. "And don't accuse Mitch again. I simply cannot believe he is a common thief." Wouldn't she have seen something suspicious in all of her time with Mitch if his motives were sinister? She had known plenty of men who were after her money. And Aunt Maude had been warning her about such men for years.

But Seth clearly had no intention of giving up his suspicions about Mitch. Bending, he picked up two pieces of her broken trunk. He glanced at the sheriff. "Sheriff, I have more than my own suspicions to go on about Mitch Lane."

Ansley listened along with the sheriff as Seth relayed

the details of meeting Mitch on the road between Martin's Creek and Prairie Chicken on the day Seth had retrieved her trunks.

"Well, doesn't the fact that he wanted to pick up my trunks for me prove he only has my best interests at heart?" She looked to the sheriff for confirmation, but his eyes were narrowed. He clearly agreed with Seth on the matter.

"Miss Potter, I think it's pretty clear Mitch Lane isn't who he claims to be. And the fact that not even the Carsons have seen him since your cabin was broken into does lead me to believe he could be guilty."

Clearly outnumbered by the men, Ansley turned her frustration on Seth. "Why didn't you come to me about this?" Ansley asked. "You said the wagon hit a hole in the road and my trunk knocked against the side of the wagon. You lied?"

"I told you the same story Lane told me when I caught him."

"You should have told me, Seth." Humiliation burned inside of her. How could she have been fooled by this man when she had seen right through the sweet-talking tactics of several men in Boston? "If I had known your suspicion of Mitch had any merit, I wouldn't have…"

Ansley closed her mouth. She was going to say she wouldn't have allowed herself to be taken in by his handsome face, gentlemanly manners and charming way of speaking to her. But doing so would have been to admit she had started to believe a man might be interested in her. With the truth discounting that, it would have been far too humiliating. Instead, she thought about what the thief, whoever he might be, had most likely been looking for.

Rising from the kitchen chair, she walked across the room and pulled the plank on the wall near the fireplace until it gave way.

Seth walked over beside her and inspected the hiding place. "I've never seen that before. Did you make it, or was it already here?"

"I found it by accident the day after I moved into the cabin." Ansley reached inside and began pulling out the velvet bags of jewelry and the clock and candelabras. She handed several to Seth and then made three trips from the wall to the table, setting the valuables on the table. "These have been in our family for many years," she explained. "They're probably what the thief was after, but I have no idea how he would have known about them."

"You brought these in your trunks?" Seth asked. Clearly he believed her foolish to have done such a thing. "You were just asking to be robbed."

"Yes, I had the trunks made specifically with false bottoms so I could transport these things to my sister."

The sheriff fingered one of the velvet bags on the table. "What other items, Miss Potter?"

"Well, it wasn't perhaps the wisest thing I could have done, but I brought several hundred dollars in cash for her. It was part of her inheritance from our aunt. And two very valuable paintings Rose had always loved."

The sheriff nodded, but clearly he wasn't finished with his questions. "Wouldn't it have been easier to bring a bank draft than to hide that much cash?"

Ansley shrugged. "I wasn't even sure a town named Prairie Chicken had a bank. I wanted her to have some of the inheritance right away. Once I spoke to Rose, I planned to find out how she wanted the rest of her share distributed, and to honor her wishes. I hung the paintings in the bedroom. They weren't disturbed. So either the thief didn't want to bother with them, or he didn't know their value."

"And the cash? I don't see it here."

"I deposited the money in the bank and paid…well, you know what I paid. When I return to Boston, I intend to set up trusts for each of the children and invest the rest of their mother's inheritance."

Seth's eyebrows rose. "You intend to give the children Rose's inheritance?"

Ansley couldn't fathom why Seth seemed so surprised by the idea.

"Of course. What else would I do with it? And so you know, I used part of their inheritance at the bank when I paid their mortgage. So it was truly their money that saved the place, not mine." Gathering up the velvet bags, Ansley headed back to the hiding place. Seth followed with the clock and candleholders.

"Don't you think we should discuss this?"

Ansley glanced at the sheriff, who shifted from one scuffed boot to the other, clearly uncomfortable now that the conversation had changed from the attempted robbery to a personal topic.

"Perhaps another time," she said softly, hoping Seth would take the hint. To her relief he did, turning his attention to the sheriff.

"So what are you going to do about Mitch Lane?"

"Now, Seth," the sheriff said. "We don't know for sure he's the one who ransacked the place. Not to mention that thanks to Miss Potter's wise actions, nothing was actually stolen."

Flushed with pleasure at the praise, Ansley smiled. "I'm sure when Mr. Lane returns he will have an explanation as to his whereabouts. After all, I just spoke with him yesterday and he seemed…well, he seemed as though he wanted to come calling on me."

Seth's frank stare annoyed her even before he spoke. "For obvious reasons."

"Perhaps a man like Mr. Lane would only be interested in my money, Seth. But it could possibly be that he knows nothing of my wealth and is innocent of your accusations."

"Then why did I catch him going through your trunk that day?"

A shrug lifted Ansley's shoulders. "I did meet him on the stage. Perhaps he truly was just doing me a kindness by retrieving my trunks and the lock broke the way he said it did."

Seth gave a snort.

Ansley's ire rose and she spun on her heel to face him. "Or perhaps the incident never occurred at all."

His eyes narrowed with an anger Ansley had yet to see. And she had seen plenty from this man standing before her. "Are you saying I'm lying?"

Ansley knew she'd been wrong to lash out at him because of her own insecurity. Once again, an apology was in order. "Of course not. I spoke out of turn."

The sheriff cleared his throat and walked toward the door. "Well, then. I reckon the only thing to do is keep our eyes open for Mr. Lane. If he shows up in town again, I'll bring him in for questioning. But unless he's caught with Miss Potter's jewelry, there's not much I can do at this time." He turned to Ansley. "Miss Potter, I suggest you find a better hiding place for your valuables. Clearly, whoever came in here looking for something to steal was focusing on those trunks and drawers and the like. But if he tries again, it wouldn't be too hard to find a loose board in the wall or floor."

"I'm sure you are right, Sheriff. I will find a more secure place."

Satisfied, he opened the door and strode outside. She expected Seth to follow him, but instead he stood, looking around the room, his eyes filled with worry. "I don't know what we pay the law for if he's not going to protect us."

His worry warmed Ansley and she touched his arm. He jerked around as though her hand was a flame, and instantly she stepped back.

"Well, at least you'll be at the boardinghouse in case he comes back."

"What do you mean? I think under the circumstances, Alice will understand if I do not come back. Besides, the midwife is staying for a couple more days."

"Ansley, you can't stay here alone when someone is clearly out to rob you. If he didn't find what he was looking for the first time, he'll be back."

"But I won't be alone. Harry won't let anyone hurt me."

He released a heavy breath. "Listen. The dog is protective. I'll give him that. And he would try to get between you and anyone bent on harming you, but even a dog the size of that one is no match for a man with a gun."

"You mean someone might shoot him?" The very idea filled Ansley with fear. And indignation that someone would dare harm her Harry.

Seth placed his hands on both her arms and looked her straight in the eye. "I know you're independent and don't like being told what to do, so believe me when I say the last thing I want is to get your back up. But you have to be smart. You're not in the city in a big house with servants now. This is a dark cabin three miles from the closest neighbor. A woman alone who has no experience living this way is just asking for trouble. Especially if that woman has already been the mark of a thief."

"But if I run away, won't that just encourage the thief to return? Or at the very least believe me to be a coward? What about making a stand to show I'm not afraid?"

His lips twitched. "You're not afraid?"

"Well, of course I am, but I'm not a coward."

"The thief obviously knew you wouldn't be home last night and came in while you were away, so I don't believe he wants to harm you. But that doesn't mean he won't if he comes back and finds you here."

A shudder made its way up Ansley's spine at the thought. And she knew full well he was still speaking of Mitch. And now that he mentioned it… "Mitch knew I was staying at the boardinghouse last night." Her voice held no inflection as she surrendered to the possibility that perhaps Seth was right. "I suppose he was just another man like those who came courting after Aunt Maude died."

"Ansley…"

She broke from his hands and shook her head. "Do not trouble yourself with my feelings about that. I have long come to terms with the fact that I am to remain unmarried. I am twenty-nine years old and I spent my youth caring for my aunt. I truly felt that was the course God expected me to stay. I just lost sight of who I truly was for a while. Of course Mitch Lane wouldn't want to court me when there are dozens of young women vying for his attention."

"I hope you know I didn't mean to imply a man couldn't care for you. I only meant I knew what he was truly after."

"Well, it doesn't matter anymore. You have shown me his true intentions and I am grateful he didn't find what he was after." She averted her gaze so he wouldn't see her lips beginning to tremble. "If you'll excuse me, I must pack some clothes if I am to stay at the boardinghouse. And we must wrap up those things. I believe Mrs. Boatwright would agree to give me some space in her safe."

Chapter 15

The Christmas Eve dance in Prairie Chicken was all anyone had talked about for the past week, and frankly Seth was tired of hearing about it. Thankfully, it was going to happen that evening. Since the boardinghouse was the only place large enough to hold the dance, Mrs. Boatwright had closed the restaurant, and the dining room was being transformed into a dance floor.

She'd been giving him orders for the past three hours and it didn't appear the end was in sight. He had moved all the tables and chairs from the dining room into the library, parlor and kitchen—anywhere he could find space out of the way.

Now it was time to set up a refreshment counter, which he'd hauled from the barn, and a platform for the musicians.

Ansley had been in and out dusting, sweeping and doing general cleaning and polishing for the event.

Since no one had seen or heard from Mitch in two weeks, Ansley decided that she would move back to the cabin for the remainder of her time in Prairie Chicken. Seth wasn't comfortable with the idea, but she wouldn't hear any arguments.

"Oh, good." Seth turned at the sound of Ansley's voice. She wore a practical gown of blue that he recognized as one of Teddy's. She had covered it with an apron. "You have everything set up. The decorating committee should be here in no time."

"Are the children excited about the dance?" Ansley asked, pushing a stray strand of hair from her forehead. It was the first time Seth had seen her in anything but fancy city clothes. He had certainly never seen her with her hair not neatly pinned. She'd never looked prettier as far as he was concerned. He grinned at her. "They're excited to wear their new dresses. They can't wait to make Sarah Wayne jealous."

The sound of Ansley's laughter echoed through the nearly empty room. "I suppose I should have held out and made them wait till Christmas morning as I planned, but every girl needs a new dress for a party. And it's only one day early."

"Did you get yourself a new dress, as well?"

"No, I hadn't planned to attend."

Her response surprised Seth. He tilted his head and frowned. "Now, why wouldn't a pretty single woman want to attend a dance?"

"Oh, Seth. Who would I dance with?" She looked away, almost as if embarrassed. "Besides," she hurried on, "Teddy is coming to town with the wagon to take me back to the cabin today so we can decorate the tree and get the house ready for tomorrow." The children had asked if they could all spend Christmas at the cabin and none of the three adults had the heart to refuse.

"If you get back in time for the dance, I'll dance with you." He figured it couldn't hurt to offer, even though he wasn't much of a dancer. Besides he didn't get the chance at the Harvest dance. After Luke Carson stole his dance with her, Ansley had been whisked away by one man after another.

"That's kind of you, but you needn't feel obligated to dance with the spinster sister-in-law of your late brother. I think I'll just go up to my room when I get back. I'm not in the mood to dance."

Seth wanted to kick himself. Clearly, she'd taken his offer as him patronizing her. How could he tell her the only reason he'd been looking forward to the dance, which he normally dreaded attending, was the thought of dancing with her? After all of their disagreements over the past several weeks, he knew there was no way she'd believe him. But that didn't mean he couldn't try. Otherwise, she'd assume she was right.

"I don't feel obligated. As a matter of fact, according to Sarah Wayne, her aunt Isabelle has decided to set her cap for me. You would be doing me a favor by allowing me to escort you to the dance."

"Seth…"

"No, I mean it. Just ask Hannah. Sarah Wayne confided that shocking bit of information to her just yesterday at school. Apparently, tonight is the night she plans to trap me with her considerable female charms." He stepped closer to her and took in her blue-green gaze. "Besides, the truth is, I have been looking forward to dancing with you."

Her face flushed as soon as he got the words out, and she smiled even as she shook her head. "As much as I would love to rescue you tonight, you've managed to remain a bachelor for—how old are you?"

"Thirty-five."

"You've managed to remain a bachelor for thirty-five years. I am confident you are skilled at skirting feminine wiles."

Reaching forward, Seth fingered the swath of hair that had fallen once more over her forehead. She'd never looked lovelier and suddenly he was at a loss for words. "Perhaps I've been waiting for the right female."

"Ah, does Isabelle Wayne have reason to hope after all?"

Seth couldn't help but laugh. "I'm afraid not."

Movement caught his attention from the corner of his eye and he glanced up to find Teddy and Jonah in the doorway.

"Hi, you two," Teddy said, sashaying into the room as she tended to do. Irritation and disappointment hit Seth. If he'd had a couple more minutes, he might have convinced Ansley to come to the dance. Teddy stopped short as Ansley took a quick step back from Seth and turned.

"Oh," Teddy said. "Did I interrupt?"

"Of course not," Ansley said. "Are you ready to go?"

"Yes and it's snowing again, so we'd best get a move on, especially if we're going to get back in time for the dance."

Seth took the opportunity presented to him. "Maybe you can talk Ansley into coming to the dance. She says she's not interested."

Teddy grinned from Seth to Ansley. "I'll do my best."

Jonah and Seth watched the women leave, then Seth clapped the boy on the shoulder. "Let's finish this so we can go home and clean up for this shindig."

"I guess Aunt Ansley is going to Boston in a week."

Seth's gut dropped. "I guess so."

Jonah sighed. "You think if I'd been nicer to her when she first came she might've stayed?"

"No. She never planned to stay. But I know she's going to miss you children." His words didn't seem to do anything to lift Jonah's spirits. "But we still have a week or so and it'll be nice to have Christmas at the cabin, won't it?"

"Yeah. Only I wish Aunt Ansley would just stay." His eyes went wide. "Couldn't she just live in the cabin? Maybe if you asked her she would stay."

"It's not safe for her to stay there alone. At least not until we catch whoever was trying to steal from her."

Jonah shrugged. "I could stay there, too. I could protect her."

"If your aunt stayed in Prairie Chicken, you would want to live with her? Why, Jonah?" Seth couldn't help but feel betrayed.

He nodded. "Aunt Ansley said one time she feels close to Mama when she is at the cabin."

"I remember."

Jonah turned his eyes to Seth. "That's how I feel when I'm there."

Ansley and Teddy walked into the cabin. The ride over in the sleigh had been cold, but Ansley's heart felt light and warm, as she looked forward to spending Christmas at the cabin with her family. She was determined not to allow herself to think about the fast-approaching day of her departure.

Harry plopped down in front of the cold fireplace, clearly glad to be home. Teddy laughed as she shoved him aside and started to build a fire. "He's found his spot in the family, hasn't he?" Teddy turned to her and frowned. "What will you do with him when you go home to Boston? Take him or leave him with us?"

"I'd like to take him, but I don't like the idea of caging him on the train for so many days. It seems cruel."

In the corner, the tree sat bare, waiting to be decorated. Ansley knew Seth and Teddy and the children had decorated a tree for their house, but they had agreed to surprise the children when they arrived at the cabin the next morning.

While Teddy built the fire, Ansley lit the stove and started coffee. While she was alone in the kitchen, she mulled over her confusing conversation with Seth earlier. Her stomach jumped and twirled as she recalled the way he had reached out and brushed her hair away from her forehead. He had looked at her so differently than he ever had before. The way no man—not even one pretending to court her—had ever looked at her. And then he'd invited her to the dance.

"There we go," Teddy said. "It'll be warm in here in no time."

The two women decorated the tree until the coffee started to boil. Then they took a break and sat down at the table, each with a steaming cup of coffee. Teddy spooned sugar into her cup. "The children are so excited we're all going to spend Christmas together at the cabin. But I know they are feeling their loss a great deal."

Ansley nodded. She, too, felt the loss. Before she had arrived in Prairie Chicken, one of her favorite things to imagine was Christmas with Rose. It had been so many years since they'd spent the holiday together, and it had always been Rose's favorite.

"I've been thinking." Teddy's voice drew Ansley from her maudlin thoughts.

"About what?" She sipped at the hot liquid.

"Why can't you stay?"

"In Prairie Chicken?"

Teddy nodded.

Ansley set her cup back on the table with a sigh. "There are reasons. Responsibilities I have taken over for Aunt Maude. She was very involved socially, especially with charities. I have always known I would be expected to carry on her work once she was gone."

"I see." Teddy seemed to let it drop, but after another swallow of coffee she shook her head. "No, I really don't. Your aunt lived her life. You should be able to live your own now."

"That *is* my life, now, Teddy."

The younger woman looked her in the eye, one eyebrow raised. "No. It's *her* life. Yours is here with your family."

"There's something I need to confess to you, and you might think differently when I do."

"If you're talking about the court hearing, I already know."

Ansley gasped. "How could you possibly?" Then she remembered, her lawyer said the papers would come to Seth and Teddy through the post. But if they knew, why would Seth still be so kind to her? "I don't understand."

"I hid the papers from Seth and decided I wouldn't tell him until I absolutely had to."

"But he would have needed to obtain a lawyer if we were going to court."

"Yes, and I spoke with one from Martin's Creek. He has been working on it."

"But that's what I wanted to tell you..."

She waved away the rest of Ansley's words. "I also received the notice saying there would be no hearing after all." She gave Ansley a quick hug. "I never thought you'd go through with it. You love the children and it's obvious they should be here. But Ansley, so should you."

"I wish I could. Truly. But it's just not possible."

"Well, I am not giving up. So be forewarned." She planted her hands on her hips and looked at the tree. "Well, this isn't going to decorate itself!"

It only took a couple of hours to finish decorating. The holly and greenery combined with the handmade decorations made the cabin look festive.

Snow was continuing to fall, and another couple of inches had thickened the ground since they arrived. The sleigh cut a neat path through the snow and the horses had no trouble getting Teddy and Ansley back to town. As they reached the boardinghouse, Teddy placed her hand on Ansley's arm. "I'm sorry for speaking out of turn. I do understand obligations. It's just that we are all going to miss you terribly when you return to Boston."

Tears sprang to Ansley's eyes. She gave her friend a quick hug. "As I will miss all of you."

Teddy collected Seth and the children so they could go home and get cleaned up for the dance. Ansley waved goodbye at the door and trudged up the stairs to her room.

A sudden headache sent her straight to her bed. She stretched out, her mind going over her conversations with Seth and then Teddy. She hadn't expected to find herself so utterly attached, not just to the children, but to the two adults, as well. She didn't know how she was ever going to leave them. She drifted to sleep, imagining a life in Prairie Chicken with her family.

When she awoke, the room was dark and music was wafting up through the floor. Her headache had gone away and she sat up. Lighting the lamp, she glanced at the clock. The dance hadn't been underway for too long. Suddenly, she decided she very much wanted to go downstairs. She wanted to see her nieces in the dresses she'd cut down for them from the gowns she'd made for Rose. She wanted to join in with the rest of the town to celebrate Christmas. And most of all, she wanted to take Seth at his word and feel his arms around her as they danced.

Chapter 16

Twenty minutes later, Ansley walked into the room of dancers. Lit by candles and a few lamps, the room held a romantic glow as the candles flickered off the walls. She spotted Teddy smiling brightly as she danced with Luke Carson. He didn't look half-bad, and from what Ansley could see in the dimly lit room, he might have even taken a bath. Mrs. Boatwright smiled and gave her a little wave from her place behind the refreshments counter. But Ansley didn't see Seth anywhere, and her stomach dipped in disappointment.

"Do you know how beautiful you are?" The whispering voice came from over her shoulder. Seth. She turned, a smile stretching her lips, and then gasped. The voice didn't belong to Seth. Fear gripped her.

"Mitch…Mr. Lane."

Ansley glanced around, frantically searching the room for Seth. Did he know Mitch Lane had come to the dance? "What are you doing here?" she asked, trying desperately to keep the tremble from her voice.

"May I have this dance?" He smiled as though he hadn't tried to rob her just a few weeks ago, and held out his hand.

The last thing Ansley wanted to do was touch hands that had ransacked her home, but since no one else seemed to notice anything awry, she didn't want to take any chances. A refusal might cause him to disappear into the snowy night and keep him from justice. "Of course." She took his hand, trying without much success to smile,

"Are you all right, Miss Potter?" he asked, a little frown creasing his brow.

"I'm just surprised to see you. It's been a while."

He led her to the dance floor and she slipped into his arms. "I do apologize for leaving without a word. I received a telegram that my father was dying and I should come home if I wanted to see him before he passed on. I left word at the Carsons' before I left."

"Oh, they must not have received your message."

His lips twitched as he looked down into her eyes. "Did you go looking for me?"

"No. The sheriff did."

"The sheriff?" He glanced around the room. "Why would the sheriff be asking about me? Were you worried something had happened to me?"

"Mr. Lane, I had no idea what had happened to you. And I certainly wasn't worried. The truth is someone entered my cabin while I was helping Alice with her children."

"What do you mean?" He frowned. He appeared to be sincerely concerned. Had Seth been wrong about him after all?

Ansley relaxed in his arms, hoping Mitch had a suitable explanation. "My home was in complete disarray, as though someone were trying to find something to steal. Seth believed...well..." Her face warmed and suddenly she wasn't so sure.

A knowing look crossed his face as he raised his eyebrows and nodded. "I see. Since the attempted robbery happened at the same time I left town, Seth assumed I had something to do with it. But you couldn't have believed such a thing." His arm tightened around her and he pulled her closer, the warmth from his hand seeping through her glove. Ansley's head began to swim.

"I didn't know what to believe. Seth's claims certainly seemed credible."

Oh, where was Seth? Why wasn't he confronting Mitch?

"How could he have accused me? I knew he was jealous that I care for you, but to try to turn you against me in this way is truly inconceivable."

He cared for her? Confusion flooded Ansley's mind. Suddenly she didn't know what to believe. Just as she was about to ask Mitch to escort her from the floor, she saw Seth out of the corner of her eye. She turned and faced him. His jaw was clenched and anger was flashing in his eyes as he strode straight for them. She gave a little gasp and Mitch turned. He stopped short, causing Ansley to stumble. She righted herself just as Seth reached them.

"So you showed your face in town again." He shook his head. "I have to say, I admire your boldness."

"It doesn't take boldness for an innocent man to come back home."

"Innocent?" A short, humorless laugh left Seth's

curled lips. "You and I both know you are far from innocent."

The music had stopped suddenly, and the three of them were the immediate focus of all eyes in the room. Ansley placed her hand on Seth's arm. "Let's go somewhere else to discuss this."

"I say we take it outside so I can beat this man the way he deserves. Then I'm taking him straight to the sheriff."

Mr. Carson seemed to appear out of nowhere. "What's the trouble here?"

Seth didn't even bother to take his gaze from Mitch. "None of your business, Carson."

"This man works for me."

"You mean the man who disappeared for two weeks?"

Mr. Carson rubbed his chin. "A man can't be faulted for going to the bedside of his dying father, now, can he?"

Seth's face blanched. "What do you mean?"

"I think Miss Potter's suggestion was apt," Mitch said. "Let's take this into another room and I can explain everything."

Ansley could tell by Seth's scowl the last thing he wanted to do was allow Mitch to explain anything. But he gave a curt nod and led the way from the room. He claimed Ansley from Mitch with a firm hand on her elbow, and the two of them walked into the parlor where they'd met that first day.

Mitch took a seat on the sofa and smiled up at Ansley as though he expected her to join him. But Ansley knew that would only antagonize Seth, so she sat on the wing chair next to the fire.

Seth poked at the fire instead of sitting with the rest

of them. He turned, folding his arms, and glared straight at Mitch. "Let's have it."

"Not that I feel you need an explanation," Mitch said, his calm voice holding a hint of steel that made Ansley shudder. "But just to put Miss Potter's mind at ease over your erroneous accusation, I'm happy to offer my side of the story."

"Go on."

"Just after I left your place…you remember Miss Potter asked that I deliver the message that Mrs. Anderson's baby had arrived and that you needed to pick up your nieces at the boardinghouse."

"I remember."

"Well, I returned to town to discover Lou Bledstoe had received a telegram for me. You may check with him if you like."

"I will." Seth's face remained immovable. "And what did this telegram say?"

"Seth…" Ansley couldn't help but feel bad for Mitch. After all, the man had just lost his father.

"Stay out of this."

Irritation flashed inside her chest. Stay out of it? "Excuse me, Seth Dobson, but since you are accusing Mitch of trying to steal from me, I don't believe you have any right to tell me to stay out of it."

"She has a point." Mitch chuckled, which only made the situation worse. Seth's hands clenched into fists and Ansley feared the two men might come to blows right there in Mrs. Boatwright's parlor.

"I want to know what was in that convenient telegram."

Releasing a sigh, Mitch crossed his ankle over his knee. "Mr. Dobson, I'm afraid the telegram wasn't convenient, nor did it hold good news. My uncle sent it to inform me my father was on his deathbed."

"And you just left with no word to anyone? Forgive me if you're being truthful, but that doesn't seem very responsible. Even for a man in grief."

Mr. Carson had been sitting silently, but now he stood to face Seth. "The fact is Mitch did leave a note on my desk to inform me he would return as soon as possible."

Seth narrowed his gaze as he turned toward Mr. Carson. "I was at your house the day after the so-called telegram arrived, Carson. Luke told me Mitch's things were absent and you didn't know where he'd gone."

Carson scowled and waved his hand. "My idiot son didn't know what he was saying."

Seth took a step forward, his fists still clenched. Surely he wouldn't hit a man twice his age. "Luke may not be a harsh man like you, but that doesn't mean he's an idiot."

"Well, that's an argument for another time. I can corroborate Mitch's story so you'll never get the sheriff to arrest him for the unfortunate incident at your brother's cabin." He looked at Mitch. "Seems we've overstayed our welcome, son."

Mitch nodded and stood. "I agree." He turned to Ansley. "May I escort you home?"

"She doesn't need you," Seth broke in before Ansley could open her mouth. "As a matter of fact, you stay away from Miss Potter."

"I think that's for Miss Potter to say."

"Yes," Ansley said. "It is for me to say. Mr. Lane, I have moved back into the boardinghouse for the remainder of my time in Prairie Chicken. So while I thank you for your generous offer to escort me home—" she gave Seth a pointed glare "—I am already home."

Mitch inclined his head and gave a short bow. "I'm relieved to know you're safe."

The snort that Seth gave was simply uncalled for. Mitch grinned at him. "I see you are not convinced of my innocence, but I am grateful that Miss Potter no longer believes I am capable of bringing any harm to her—or stealing from her."

"Good night, Mr. Lane. Thank you for the lovely dance. Please allow me to escort you to the door."

She slipped her hand inside the crook of his extended arm and they walked through the foyer to the door.

"I hope I may call on you now that this little misunderstanding has been cleared up. I would like to take up where we left things before I had to go away."

"But my circumstances have not changed. I will be leaving town soon. I see no reason to give you false hope."

His face darkened for an instant, but brightened again so quickly Ansley almost believed she had imagined the change. Almost. Her stomach twisted with uncertainty and she couldn't help but feel as though Mitch Lane was not all he appeared to be.

Seth stood in helpless fury and watched Ansley leave the room with that low-down snake, Mitch Lane. He knew jealousy when it rose up and he had to admit the feeling was present inside of him. But that wasn't all he felt. No matter what Mitch Lane claimed, he had no doubt the man was behind the attempted robbery at the cabin.

He waited for her by the door leading back into the dance. The last song was playing and they would be dismissed soon. But he hoped for one dance with her before the evening ended.

She came toward him, her lavender silk gown kissing the floor as she walked. When she saw him, her eyes clouded. The look could only mean one thing.

"Oh, Ansley. Surely you didn't believe any of that."

"Do not presume to tell me what to think, Seth Dobson. And how dare you order Mitch Lane to stay away from me?" Her voice shook as she spoke.

"How dare I? How can you even ask me that? Clearly, you don't feel safe as you thought you were, since you told him you weren't going to move back to the cabin. Didn't you insist on moving back there for the week?" He slapped his palms against the sides of his legs. "I'm trying to protect you."

"Do you truly believe I need protection from him, even after he offered a perfectly reasonable explanation for his absence?" Her chest rose and fell quickly, as though she were out of breath. "Honestly, Seth. All you have to do is confirm his statement with Mr. Bledstoe at the telegraph office."

The music inside the room ended and Seth's heart sank. "Well, I suppose the dance is over. The girls fell asleep in a corner an hour ago."

Ansley's expression softened considerably at the mention of Hannah and Lily. "May I help you get them to the sleigh?"

"Teddy can help." Seth could have kicked himself for saying that. He hadn't meant to be spiteful, but the way her expression fell once more, he realized she assumed he had. "You can if you'd like, though. At least come and kiss them good-night. I'll let them know tomorrow that you did."

Her eyes widened and she smiled. "Seth, what if the girls spend the night here with me? I mean, that way you won't need to get them out in the snow and cold. And I haven't spent nearly enough time with them lately."

Teddy appeared in the doorway. "What are you two arguing about now? I saw Mitch Lane showed up. What's his flimsy excuse for being gone all this time?"

Seth gave her a silencing stare. "We'll talk about it later."

"You'd best come help me with the girls. I've been trying to wake them, but they're not budging." She grinned. "They sleep as dead as you do."

"Ansley would like the girls to spend the night here with her."

"That's a lovely idea. Then we wouldn't have to get them all bundled up and take them out in the cold. You sure you don't mind?"

"Of course not."

"I'll be by here early tomorrow so we can all go to the cabin."

Under Mrs. Boatwright's watchful eye, Seth carried Hannah upstairs while Ansley followed with Lily. They tucked the girls into Ansley's bed and she walked with him into the hall, closing the door behind her. In the hallway, Seth searched her face. "I'm sorry for the way this night turned out."

She leaned back against the door. "I shouldn't have gone down to the dance."

"You look beautiful tonight." Though as far as Seth was concerned, she had looked just as beautiful earlier in her borrowed muslin dress, with her hair in disarray. He hated the sadness in her eyes, especially knowing he was the cause of it. "I could have handled things better tonight. I'm sorry."

"You believe Mitch, then?"

"No. I don't know about the telegram or about his

father dying. But I know he's a dangerous man with dishonorable intentions."

"There is something—not right. I just can't put my finger on what."

"Do you mean to say you didn't believe his story?"

"I wanted to." She gave him a rueful smile. "After all, if he isn't telling the truth, then I'm a fool for believing he cares about me. But there's something dangerous about him. And I think he might have followed me here from Boston."

Seth took hold of her arm and searched her eyes. "What do you mean?"

"The day we arrived, I kept thinking he looked familiar. But there are so many handsome older men in my circles in Boston, I thought perhaps I was imagining it. Still, I can't quite shake the feeling that I saw him several times during the train ride."

"Why didn't you tell me this before?" Seth dropped her arm but kept his gaze firmly on hers.

"I don't know. I thought I was just being silly. Why don't you find out from Mr. Bledstoe where the telegram came from?"

"I intend to. In the meantime, will you please be careful around him? Until we know for sure, don't allow him to escort you anywhere."

"You're asking me this time instead of ordering?" Ansley's smile softened her words.

"I'm not just asking, I'm begging, Ansley. If Mitch is the sort of man I believe him to be, he's not only a common thief, but a dangerous one."

Ansley nodded. "I'll be careful. I promise."

Relief coursed through him. It was all Seth could do to keep from grabbing her and pulling her close. If only he didn't have to leave. He would definitely feel much better if he could be there to protect her.

"I'll see you in the morning."

Seth nodded, knowing she was saying good-night. "I'll be here early."

Reluctantly he walked away, glad that at least Mitch Lane would have no opportunity between now and the morning to do any harm.

Chapter 17

Ansley couldn't breathe. She awakened suddenly, her eyes opening to the blackness of her bedroom. Then she realized a dark figure was standing over her, his hand covering her mouth. "Shh. Don't force me to wake the girls." Slowly, he took his hand away.

Fear licked at her belly. "Mitch," she whispered.

He tossed her dressing gown from the bottom of the bed and turned around. "Don't try anything."

"What do you want?" She quickly slipped the gown over her nightdress, painfully aware that no man had ever seen her in such scanty attire.

Mitch's fingers dug into her arm as he reached out and grabbed her. He led her quickly through the door, down the steps and into the kitchen. "Where is it?"

"Where is what?"

"Ansley, don't play ignorant. I haven't the time nor the patience for it."

Ansley shook her head as she stared at him, lit as he was only by the moon glinting off the snow. "So it was you, after all."

"Yes, and as soon as your dear Seth confirms with Bledstoe that I never received a telegram, I'll be asked to answer a lot of questions I don't want to answer. It would be much better for me if I'm long gone before that happens."

Ansley peered closer at him. He no longer wore his fancy suit. Instead, he was dressed in denim trousers, a wool shirt and a coat. Dress so common, her memory finally conjured him.

"You worked at the shop where I ordered my trunks!"

"Finally remembered me?" He gave a short, bitter laugh. "I'm surprised a society woman even bothered to look at my face."

"I saw you twice. Once at the shop and again when you delivered the trunks to me." She narrowed her gaze. "You came all the way from Boston?"

"You're not extremely smart, Ansley. The day I brought your trunks to you, all the pieces of jewelry and the other things you were bringing with you were just sitting out on the table. And as you were paying me for my delivery, you stopped your maid and asked her to look for the false bottoms of the trunks and place those things inside. I planned to steal them along the way, but first the train kept the luggage guarded too well. And then the stagecoach driver wouldn't allow you to weigh down the coach with the trunks."

"And the day Seth found you with them?"

"Well, if he'd been ten minutes later, we wouldn't be having this conversation."

Fury lit inside of Ansley. "So you played on my affections, to what end? Did you intend to marry me for my money?"

"Well, that wouldn't have been my first choice." He gave a sardonic smile. "You're a bit long in the tooth for a bride."

Ansley's cheeks flooded with heat as humiliation spread through her chest.

"Not that you aren't still a very beautiful woman. You are. But if I were to marry, of course it would be to someone much younger, without such an independent streak."

"I wouldn't marry you, anyway." It was a childish thing to say, but Ansley didn't care. Mitch's chuckle only increased her rage.

"What have you done with the clock and jewels, Ansley?"

"You went to the trouble of procuring a position with Mr. Carson and following me all this way just for a few jewels and a clock?"

"The position with Mr. Carson was a lucky break. His son was on the stage, remember? Otherwise, I'd have never known the old man was looking for a hired gun. Anyway, I meant to steal them much sooner. But your Seth revealed my hand on the road that day. So I was forced to trifle with your affections. I truly regret the necessity of that."

"Don't flatter yourself, Mr. Lane. I was never all that interested."

"Be that as it may, you've learned all my secrets. I must be going soon, so if we can move this along, I'd like to collect my things and go."

"Your things? You mean my things. You're nothing but a thief, and I can't believe I ever defended you to Seth."

"Well, perhaps you'll be wiser next time."

Next time? Ansley nearly sighed in relief. Did this mean he didn't intend to kill her? So far, he hadn't threatened her with bodily harm and he hadn't drawn his pistol.

"Enough stalling, Ansley. Where are they?"

His voice had grown impatient and she knew she had no choice. Her mind went to the jewels she and Rose had grown up admiring, the clock and candelabras that had been their mother's—a gift from their father the day they had wed. The jewels, she wouldn't miss so much. After all, she certainly hadn't been the one to wear them. But the clock and candlesticks had sentimental value. "They're in Mrs. Boatwright's safe."

"And that would be located where?"

Ansley hesitated. She knew she was the only person Mrs. Boatwright had trusted with the safe and combination since her own sister had gone on to be with Jesus. "In the library."

He took hold of her arm again. "Let's go."

The embers of last night's fire still glowed, but they certainly didn't provide enough light for Ansley to see the numbers on the safe. She turned to him. "I'll need a light."

He nodded and reached for a candle on the mantel. "This will have to do. I'm not lighting a lamp."

"I'll also need that stool to stand on." She was taller than most women, but she was still not tall enough to accomplish this horrid task without a lift. He set the small stool next to her and offered his hand to help her up. Ansley glanced at the hand and jerked her head, using the mantel to steady herself. She reached above the fireplace and removed the large painting that covered the wall safe. She handed the painting to Mitch.

Mitch released a soft laugh as he took it and set it against the bricks. "I should have known."

It didn't take Ansley long to open the safe. Her stomach sank as she slowly pulled out the bags of jewelry and handed them to the thief. "Now the clock and candelabras," he ordered.

Ansley did as he instructed and then started to close the safe.

"Wait." Mitch grinned at her. "I'm sure a woman such as Mrs. Boatwright has something inside there that might interest a man like me."

"A low-down thief, you mean? An outlaw? A good-for-nothing…"

"I get your meaning, Ansley. Just empty the safe."

Ansley stepped down from the stool and folded her arms. "I will not assist you in robbing Mrs. Boatwright."

He scowled. He set the candleholder on the table next to his spoils and moved forward, reaching into the safe. Candlelight flickered off the shiny, heavy gold clock. Ansley saw her next movement an instant before she acted. Without giving herself an opportunity to change her mind, she snatched up the clock with both hands, raised it high and brought it down on the back of Mitch's neck. He turned and she gasped. "You little…"

She hit him again, this time across the side of his head, and he dropped to the floor, unconscious. Praying she hadn't killed him, Ansley grabbed the key from the desk in the library and hurried out the door. She heard him moan just as she closed the doors and turned the lock to keep him inside until she could alert the sheriff.

Hurrying upstairs, she knocked on Mrs. Boatwright's door. The old woman answered, her thick silver braid slung across one shoulder. "Ansley. What on earth?"

Ansley quickly explained what had happened, and then hurried to her room to dress. Thankfully, the girls slept on as she left the room, carefully closing the door after her, and slipped out into the cold night. It wouldn't take long for Mitch to wake up and shoot the lock on the library door. Deciding it would take longer to saddle Bella than to trudge through the foot of snow on the ground, she crossed the street and hurried as fast as she could toward the sheriff's office. She was not altogether sure whether he slept there or closed the office at night. She was shivering and wet from her knees down by the time she tried the door, and gratefully she found it open. The sheriff sat up instantly in his cot in one of the cells, pistol drawn.

Ansley quickly told him what had happened. He shrugged into his coat, clamped his hat down on his head and walked her back to the boardinghouse. They found Mrs. Boatwright and Alice in the library, the door busted through as Ansley had feared could happen. Mitch was long gone.

"Don't worry," the sheriff said. "He can't hide his footprints in this snow. Just pray the sky stays clear."

The girls ran down the steps as soon as Seth walked into the foyer of the boardinghouse Christmas morning. And while the girls were glowing with excitement, one look at Ansley told Seth she hadn't slept the night before. He frowned as he walked through the foyer and noted the library door in splinters. "What happened?"

Casting a cautious glance toward the girls, Ansley shook her head and then smiled at their nieces. "Girls, Mrs. King has breakfast for you in the dining room. But hurry now, so we can get to the cabin."

As the children left through the doorway to the

kitchen, Seth turned back to Ansley. They walked together into the library. "Mitch broke in last night."

Mrs. Boatwright entered the library. "He would have gotten away with a lot more if Ansley here hadn't knocked him over the head with that clock."

Ansley's face flushed. "He still got away."

"Only with what he could stuff in his pockets. He had to leave most of the jewelry and the bigger items."

Seth stared from one woman to the other until his gaze rested on Ansley. "Start at the beginning."

Ire surged through him as he realized Mitch had entered Ansley's bedroom and forced her to open the safe, but it was replaced with pride at her bravery. "You haven't heard from the sheriff since last night?"

"No. But he doesn't think Mitch will be able to get away, with his tracks so easy to read in this snow."

"I suppose I should go out and help him find Mitch." As a matter of fact, the more help the sheriff had, the greater chance the thief would be brought to justice without delay. Once that happened, Seth could stop worrying about Ansley.

"If that's what you think is best," Ansley said with unusual compliance. "The children will be disappointed."

Seth knew she was right. This Christmas, more than any other, meant a great deal to the children. It was their first without their parents and their first with their new aunt. He couldn't disappoint them. He would have to put his trust in God and the sheriff.

While the girls ate their breakfasts, Ansley returned upstairs to pack up their things and collect the children's gifts. Mrs. Boatwright motioned him toward a chair and he sat. "You know I don't generally like to meddle in matters that aren't my business."

Seth tensed. When a person started a conversation with those words, it was pretty obvious she was, indeed, about to meddle.

"Are you going to let that girl get away?"

"Now, Mrs. Boatwright."

"Far be it from me to criticize, but if you let her go back to Boston, I think you'll be making a big mistake."

"I'm not sure what you want me to do about it, ma'am." Seth glanced at the door. Where was Ansley?

She scowled at him and stood up. "Fine, play dumb and lose her." With that she left the library without looking back.

Moments later, Seth bundled the girls into the sleigh and helped Ansley into the back. Then they headed out of town, sliding through the snow.

Ansley turned to him. "You don't think Mitch would come back for the rest of the things in that safe, do you?"

"You mean he was biding his time until you and I left and the sheriff was off somewhere looking for him?"

"It seems reasonable." Her eyes were clouded over with worry and Seth felt a growing concern that she was most likely right.

"I'm turning around."

She placed her hand on his arm. "The children."

Seth nudged the horses to a faster pace and pulled up to the cabin a few minutes later. He and Ansley helped the girls inside and he quickly explained the circumstances to Teddy. "I'll be back as soon as I can."

Ansley followed. "I'm going with you."

He opened his mouth to argue, but she raised her hand. "Don't even try to stop me."

They raced back to town and arrived just in time to see Mitch, bag in hand, hopping on his horse. "Go after him!" Ansley's voice carried across the stillness of the snow-covered town and Mitch turned. He tried to urge his horse to go faster, but the snow was too deep. In the sleigh, they easily caught up to him. Seth tossed Ansley the reins and stood as they came alongside the thief. He jumped, knocking Mitch from his horse, and the two men tumbled into the snow. Seth made short work of the ensuing struggle. Pulling the string out of the bag of stolen items, Seth bound Mitch's hands behind his back.

While Ansley hurried back to the boardinghouse to check on Mrs. Boatwright and the other women and children, Seth hustled Mitch to the sheriff's office. As they walked in the door, the sheriff said, "I was just about to head back out to look for him. Glad I'll be able to spend Christmas with the wife, after all."

Seth turned the man over and watched with satisfaction as the sheriff shoved him into a cell and closed the door with a resounding clang.

Mitch released a short laugh. "What made you decide to come back to the boardinghouse?" he asked.

"Ansley. She figured you might try to come back for the rest of her belongings after we were gone."

He shook his head. "She's a smart one. Strong, too." He touched the long bruise at the side of his face. "After you marry her, don't cross her."

Seth scowled. First Mrs. Boatwright, now this inconsequential thief? "She's going back to Boston in a week. Unwed."

Mitch grinned and stretched out on the cot. "We'll see."

Chapter 18

Much to Ansley's relief, Mitch had harmed no one within the boardinghouse. But Mrs. Boatwright was fit to be tied. "Imagine that man coming here twice to rob us. I hope Seth Dobson hurt him well and good."

"It wasn't much of a fight." Ansley couldn't help but catch Alice's eye. She grinned. "Apparently Mitch isn't too fearsome unless you're a woman."

Mrs. Boatwright gave an indelicate snort. "You got the best of him. I never much cared for a man who couldn't take care of himself." She angled a sly gaze at Ansley. "Seth is one of the good ones. A real man."

Ansley captured her in a quick hug. "You'll get no argument from me on that."

"Then don't go back to Boston."

"I have to. It's my home."

"Seems to me you have children and a man who loves you right here."

Shocked, Ansley laughed. "Mrs. Boatwright! I admit

we have stopped butting heads over the children, but Seth has never said one word to me of love."

"Hogwash. Men don't love in word—they love in deed. And he's proven he cares for you."

The bell above the front door jangled, signaling Seth's return. Ansley silently implored Mrs. Boatwright not to say any more.

A few minutes later, Seth and Ansley waved goodbye from the sleigh. Seth flicked the reins, nudging the horses forward. "I so wish Alice had heard from her husband before Christmas, as she had expected."

"There's been no word?" Seth asked.

"He responded to the telegram I sent when the baby was born, but there's been nothing since."

"Well, Mrs. Boatwright will take good care of them until he comes." He paused and they rode along in silence for a few minutes until he let out a laugh. "You know, that Mrs. Boatwright is a good woman, but she actually told me I should not let you go back to Boston. Seemed to think we should just get married."

Ansley's stomach dipped at his words. "That's…so silly. She told me essentially the same thing."

Turning her head, she watched the snow-covered trees racing by. Of course it was silly. Silly to think a man like this—a real man, one of the good ones—could possibly love her so much he didn't want her to leave.

Awkward silence carried them along the path until they reached the cabin. From within, the sound of Rose's piano carried to where they had stopped in the snow. When Seth made no move to get out of the sleigh, Ansley turned to find him watching her.

"Do you think it's silly?" he asked.

"Well, of course."

With a nod, he wrapped the reins and hopped down.

As Ansley stepped from the sleigh, he took her hand and kept hold of it. Ansley searched his face. "Don't you?"

Seth walked her toward the house and up onto the porch, but he stopped short before going inside. "You know, Miss Potter. We never had that dance together last night."

Ansley laughed. "Well, that's one way to change the subject."

Seth's face remained sober. "May I have this dance?"

"Out here?"

"There's music. And the porch is pretty much cleared." He didn't wait. He drew her into his arms and they moved to the music, Seth never taking his eyes from hers.

"I don't think it's silly at all," he said, his voice low and husky. "The fact is, if you leave, I'll come after you and camp on your doorstep every night until you agree to come back here to live with us."

"Seth…"

"I know I haven't always been kind or fair. I know I haven't treated you the way I should have, but if you'll have me, we can put all that in the past. Obviously I can't give you the life of luxury you're accustomed to. But…"

Tears clogged Ansley's throat, but she could listen to no more. She reached up and pressed her fingers to his lips. "I don't need a life of luxury. I don't need Boston, and I don't need a man who doesn't stand up to me. Seth Dobson, I just need you."

Seth's lips claimed hers almost before the words had left them. And even in the cold Kansas wind, Ansley had never felt so warm.

The door flew open and the three children, followed by Teddy, rushed onto the porch. "I told you, Lily!" Hannah shouted. "I told you God always answers Christmas prayers."

Lily planted her hands on her plump little hips. "You didn't tell me. I told you!"

Seth swung Lily into his arms. "What are you girls talking about?"

"Last night we prayed that Aunt Ansley would stay here and marry you, Uncle Seth."

Seth shifted Lily to one side and held out his other hand to Ansley. "And God did answer your prayer. As a matter of fact, He answered mine, too."

Ansley slipped her hand into his and they walked inside together. There were details of her life in Boston she would have to attend to, but for now, she intended to enjoy the first of many Christmases with her family.

* * * * *